CANZONE VILLANESCHE ALLA NAPOLITANA
AND VILLOTTE

RECENT RESEARCHES IN THE MUSIC OF THE RENAISSANCE • VOLUME XXX

Adrian Willaert and His Circle

CANZONE VILLANESCHE ALLA NAPOLITANA AND VILLOTTE

Edited by Donna G. Cardamone

A-R EDITIONS, INC. • MADISON

For my parents

ISSN 0486-123X

ISBN 0-89579-108-0

Library of Congress Cataloging in Publication Data:

Main entry under title:

Canzone villanesche alla napolitana and villotte.

   (Recent researches in the music of the Renaissance ;
v. 30)
   For cantus, altus, tenor, and bassus; includes arrange-
ments of some of the works for lute or for voice and
vihuela (tablature and staff notation)
   The original works edited from eds. published by
G. Scotto or A. Gardane, Venice, 1541-1566.
   Italian words; also printed as texts with English
translations on p. xxvi.
   Bibliography: p. xxiv.
   Contains works by Willaert, P. Cambio, F. Corteccia,
and F. Silvestrino; includes 3-part works by G. D. da
Nola on which 4 of the 4-part works are based.
   1. Vocal quartets, Unaccompanied—Scores. 2. Vocal
trios, Unaccompanied—Scores. 3. Lute music, Arranged.
4. Songs (High voice) with vihuela. I. Willaert,
Adrian, 1490?-1562. Works, vocal. Selections. 1978.
II. Cardamone, Donna G. III. Series.
M2.R2384   vol. 30   [M140]   [M1579.3]   [M1579.4]   [M1623]
ISBN 0-89579-108-0   780'.903'1s   [784'.3064]   78-10400

Contents

THREE-VOICE SONG MODELS

LUTE INTABULATIONS

INTABULATIONS FOR VOICE AND VIHUELA

Preface

Introduction

In his patriarchal position as *maestro di cappella* of San Marco in Venice (1527-62), Adrian Willaert held a place of honor at the center of a closely knit circle of composers, printers, and theorists. Willaert's sphere of influence attracted the patronage of the noblemen Neri Capponi and Marco Trivisano for whom he organized brilliant musical evenings which acquired great fame and had a lasting effect on the private musical life of the city.[1] "One of the rarest intellects ever to have practiced composition,"[2] Willaert was the teacher and friend of relatively unknown or young composers from Italy and his native Flanders whose works he introduced and promoted in his publications. Among those to draw support from his protection were Perissone Cambio (Piersson), Francesco Corteccia, and Francesco Silvestrino. Willaert included some of their compositions in his only collection of *canzone villanesche* which Gerolamo Scotto and Antonio Gardane published in a series of revised editions and reprints between 1544 and 1563, and which shall be referred to here as Willaert's series.

The present edition contains all the four-voice compositions by Willaert and his disciples which were collected and published in the series under Willaert's name. Although the majority are *canzone villanesche*, Willaert added a few *villotte* and *canzoni* (nos. [1] - [20]); hence this collection provides a representative view of the genres of secular vocal music current in the 1540s. The three-voice *villanesche* by Gian Domenico da Nola which Willaert and Silvestrino reworked for four voices have also been included (nos. [21] - [24]) for purposes of comparison, as have intabulations of the four-voice *villanesche* (nos. [25] - [32]) made shortly after the first editions of the collection had been published.

As interest in the three-voice *frottola* declined in the Veneto region, the popular style continued to be cultivated in polyphonic elaborations of traditional melodies called *villotte*. About 1541, northern composers found still another source of inspiration in a unique form of *musica popolaresca* imported from Naples, where it had been developed by Gian Domenico da Nola. Nola's volumes of rustic songs for three voices in the Neapolitan style (*canzone villanesche alla napolitana*) were well-received by Willaert and his disciples who arranged some of them for four voices in madrigalesque polyphony to accommodate the needs and taste of the prosperous Venetian society. The Italian lutanists Giulio Abondante and Domenico Bianchini and the Spaniard Diego Pisador selected the most attractive compositions from Willaert's collection and intabulated them for the increasing numbers of amateur lute and vihuela players. The link in the chain of circumstances which inspired this corpus of vocal and instrumental compositions was Adrian Willaert, the first composer to fully recognize the potential of Nola's Neapolitan style. The present volume aims to illustrate Willaert's central role in generating a new direction for Italian popular music; this anthology of pieces taken from Willaert's series of related editions draws together a varied group of composers and arrangers who, under the impact of his leadership, created an artistic bridge between northern and southern lyric traditions. A list of all printed sources from which this repertory of interrelated vocal and instrumental compositions derives and the Key to Abbreviations used hereafter to identify them appear on p. xxiv.

The Circle About the Master

Nola

Gian Domenico del Giovane da Nola (ca. 1520-92) was virtually an unknown composer when his *canzone villanesche* attracted the attention of the Venetian musical community. Two books of his Neapolitan songs were printed together in one volume by Scotto in 1541 (not extant); Gardane divided the corpus into two separate books for reissue in 1545. Nola was probably the pupil of another *villanesca* composer, Giovan Tommaso di Maio, whom he succeeded in 1563 as *maestro di cappella* at the SS. Annunziata in Naples and with whom he may have studied at the small music school connected to the church.[3]

Corteccia

The title page of the first publication in Willaert's series, which Scotto brought out in 1544 (W1544 Sc), advertised the compositions by Willaert and "some other *canzone villanesche alla napolitana* for four voices composed by M. Francesco Corteccia, never before seen nor printed, and newly brought to light." By 1544 a large bundle of Corteccia's music had evidently reached Scotto. On September 5 of that year, Scotto was granted a ten-year privilege by the Venetian Senate to print two books of Corteccia's four-voice madrigals and Willaert's volume:

> Let Gerolamo Scotto be granted the right to print the following books, *Li madrigali del Corteggia libro primo et secundo, le canzone alla neapolitana de M. Adriano . . .* and let no one be permitted to print them or to have them printed either in this city or in any of our domains, nor print them elsewhere for sale during the next ten years without his permission.[4]

An inventory dated 1544 of the holdings of the Accademia Filarmonica Library in Verona contains an item which suggests that an entire volume of Corteccia's dialect songs was once bound together with his madrigals: "Canzoni napolitane et madrigali di Francesco Corteccia legati insieme."[5] In his last will and testament of June 5, 1571, Corteccia left all his prints and manuscripts including "canzoni, mottecti, et responsi" to a canon at San Lorenzo in Florence.[6] Unfortunately the volume (or volumes) of *canzoni* has never been found. Whether Corteccia ever met Willaert is not known, since he spent his entire life in Florence (1502-71) where he was engaged in writing compositions for the court of Duke Cosimo I and various churches where he was employed.[7] Corteccia may have established his Venetian connections through two Florentines living in Venice who were acquainted with one another, Neri Capponi (Willaert's patron) and Antonfrancesco Doni. Doni, an amateur musician and writer, had come to Venice early in 1544 and had established a business relationship and personal friendship with Scotto, who in that year printed his *Dialogo della musica* and *Lettere*.[8]

Silvestrino

Of the three composers sponsored by Willaert, Francesco Silvestrino "ditto Chechin" appears to have been the least successful. He may have been the viola player, M. Chechin, whom Doni names in the *Dialogo della musica*.[9] Three of his *villanesche* appeared in the edition of Willaert's series printed in 1545; the number was reduced to one in the reprint of 1548 to make space for Willaert's "Canzon di Ruzante" and Perissone Cambio's "Buccucia dolce."

Perissone

Perissone was a well-known figure in Venetian musical circles by this time, as opposed to Silvestrino who had not attracted sufficient attention to warrant continued publication of his works. Perissone was employed as a singer at San Marco under

Willaert during the 1540s, having come to Venice from Flanders. In a privilege granted by the Venetian Senate on June 2, 1545, for his *Madrigali sopra li sonnetti di Petrarca*, he was listed as "Perissone fiamengo."[10] He was one of the interlocutors in the second part of Doni's *Dialogo della musica* in which the activities of a fictitious Venetian musical academy are recreated. Doni praised his singing ability thus: "Messer Perissone will then sing; you will hear a fine voice and a perfect style."[11] As a professional singer, Perissone participated in events sponsored by an informal music club (*ridotto*) which met regularly at the home of a Venetian patrician, Antonio Zantani.[12] His reputation as a *villanesca* composer was acknowledged by Baldissera Donato, a Venetian composer and one of Zantani's coterie, who included two of Perissone's pieces in his collection of 1550. One is the gently erotic "Zuccharo porti a ssa buccucia" in the same vein as "Buccucia dolce." Monsignore Gerolamo Fenaruolo, a founder of the Accademia della Fama, and Domenico Venier, founder of the Accademia Veniera, mourned Perissone's death (ca. 1574) with an exchange of sonnets which contain puns on his name:

> By special favor there was once granted only to us a very rare, distinguished and unique talent . . . When may we be granted equal change in exchange for the great Cambio? (Venier)[13]

> In one blow the highly prized sound perished and in his behalf I send sorrowful laments (a bitter exchange) to every corner of the Adriatic. (Fenaruolo)[14]

The Intabulators

Like Perissone, the lutanist Giulio Abondante was invited to perform for the *ridotto* of Antonio Zantani.[15] Orazio Toscanella, a frequent guest at these gatherings, recalled that Zantani paid Abondante for his services and that he was "a lute player without equal."[16] Another lutanist, Domenico Bianchini "detto Rossetto" mentioned in Doni's *Dialogo* and Calmo's *Lettera a la signora Calandra*,[17] made the first known intabulation of a *canzone villanesca*. Bianchini included Willaert's "Madonna io non lo so" (no. [26]) in his first lute book of 1546, dedicated to "Li signori Marcadanti di Fontego Allemani," German merchants living in Venice.[18] Abondante included four intabulations of Willaert's *villanesche* in his second lute book of 1548 which he dedicated to the nobleman Alessandro Ramuino. In Spain Willaert's *villanesche* were promoted by Diego Pisador (b. 1509-d. after 1557), compiler and printer of the *Libro de música de vihuela* (1552). The seventh part of this large volume was devoted to Pisador's own intabulations of current Italian compositions. The numerous errors in the vihuela book, which he printed privately in his home at Salamanca after working on it for fifteen years, lead to the belief that Pisador was probably an amateur musician.[19]

The Venetian Musical Environment

We do not know if Willaert composed his popular songs specifically for performance in the academic circles whose musical activities he organized. Yet we can presume that *canzone villanesche* and *villotte* imparted an element of lighthearted pleasure to these musical gatherings as an agreeable alternative to the polite sociability and literary ambition of the madrigal.[20] Judging from the wide distribution of *villanesca* books in Venice and outlying areas, Neapolitan dialect songs rivaled the madrigal in popularity. Inventories of the Accademia Filarmonica Library in Verona indicate that a considerable number of *villanesca* books by Willaert and his disciples were retained throughout the sixteenth century for the enjoyment of the membership.[21] According to contemporary accounts, popular music was highly prized as a form of amusement and relaxation. In the opinion of the humanist philosopher Alessandro Piccolomini, Neapolitan tunes in particular, as opposed to their more lively northern counterparts, could stimulate the sweet sensation of relaxed pleasure:

> Take for example those musical tunes which are used in Lombardy [*villotte*?]. They inflame the soul and fill it with a certain eagerness and enthusiasm; they move the whole body to external movement, almost by force. On the contrary, the Neapolitan tunes sweeten and mollify the soul and in part render it effeminate and soft.[22]

Venice, like every major city in Italy, had its renowned and accomplished courtesans whose homes were often the scene of brilliant literary and musical events. Many of these women rose to the level of *oneste cortigiane* by cultivating the protection and admiration of men of high birth through whom they maintained a respectable position in society. In order to avoid sinking to a more wanton way of life, they were expected to foster the literary, musical, and conversational interests of their well-educated noble consorts. For the talented courtesan, musical performance could be a widely recognized artistic achievement. According to Doni, the remarkable Polissena Pecorina was a welcome guest in the Venetian *ridotto* of Neri Capponi: "There is here a lady (the consort of a compatriot of mine) so clever and cultivated that I cannot find words to praise her. One evening I heard a concert of *violoni*

and voices at which she sang and played with other outstanding personalities; the perfect master of this music was Adriano Willaert."[23] Willaert dedicated the first edition of the *Musica Nova* to that outstanding interpreter of his music, La Pecorina.[24]

Even less-accomplished courtesans commanded the interest of devoted noble admirers. As a matter of routine these women, like their more exalted counterparts, were instructed in the arts (or better, professional tricks) of their trade. In their circles, singing, dancing, and playing musical instruments were overt forms of invitation. "The sounds, songs, and literature which women know are the keys which open the door to their modesty," in the opinion of the Venetian libertine, Pietro Aretino.[25] Popular songs, composed to trite and inconsequential love poetry, were well-suited to the hedonistic atmosphere created by this class of courtesan. For example, a typical evening at the home of Marietta Schiavona, a Venetian courtesan, featured a young girl's seductive rendition of *napolitane*:

> Not long after, three very beautiful young girls between the ages of sixteen and eighteen appeared. They were dressed and adorned so magnificently that not only did they seem like three earthly women, but also truly like three goddesses descended from heaven. . . . [After every gentleman had made his choice] Marsilio, who was a very well-mannered courtier, called one of his servants and told him to prepare a splendid little meal of sweets and fruits as speedily as possible. Then he took his girl by the hand and made her sit in the company of the others. They discussed many pleasant and amorous things together. One of the girls, seeing that the *clavicembalo* was open, began to play and to sing some very nice *napolitane* so sweetly and with so much suavity and harmony, that she greatly astounded the gentlemen. Indeed, could they have refused the ones they had chosen first without losing their self-respect, they would have competed with one another to choose this one who sang and played so graciously.[26]

The widespread appeal of light music in Venice distressed the moralists, among them Nicola Vicentino, priest, theorist, and pupil of Willaert, who said:

> One should not be surprised if, in these times, music is not held in high esteem, since it has been applied to low things, such as *balli*, *napolitane*, and to *villotte*, and other ridiculous things, contrary to the opinion of the ancients who reserved it only for the singing of hymns of the gods and of the great deeds of men.[27]

Napolitane (i.e., *canzone villanesche* and *villanelle*) were repeatedly condemned by pessimists and antihe-

Figure 1. Classification of Compositions in Willaert's Series

Incipit	Genre	Location of the tune	Mode of the tune	Final	Clefs
[1] A quand'a quand'haveva una vicina (Adriano)	villanesca	cantus	Ionian	F	SAAB
[2] Buccucia dolce chiù che canamielle (Piersson)	villanesca	migrant*	Ionian	F	SATB
[3] Cingari simo venit'a giocare (Adriano)	mascherata alla napolitana	tenor	Hypodorian	G	SATB
[4] Le vecchie per invidia sono pazze (Corteccia)	villanesca	cantus	Ionian	C	SATB
[5] Madonna mia famme bon' offerta (Adriano)	villanesca	migrant*	Ionian	F	SMABar
[6] Madonna mia io son un poverello (Anon.)	villanesca	cantus	Dorian	D	SATB
[7] Madonn'io non lo so perchè lo fai (Adriano)	villanesca	tenor	Hypodorian	G	SATB
[8] Madonn'io t'haggi amat'et amo assai (Corteccia)	villanesca	cantus	Hypodorian	G	SATB
[9] O bene mio fam'uno favore (Adriano)	villanesca	cantus	Hypodorian	D	MMTB
[10] O Dio si vede chiaro cha per te moro (Silvestrino)	villanesca	tenor	Dorian	D	VMAB
[11] O dolce vita mia che t'haggio fatto (Adriano)	villanesca	tenor	Hypodorian	D	VSMT
[12] Occhio non fu giamai che lachrimasse (Adriano)	canzone	tenor	Dorian	D	V[S]ST
[13] Quando di rose d'oro (Adriano)	canzone	tenor	Dorian	D	V[S]ST
[14] Se mille volte ti vengh'a vedere (Silvestrino)	villanesca	tenor	Dorian	G	VMAB
[15] Sempre mi ride sta donna da bene (Adriano)	villanesca	tenor	Ionian	C	VMMBar
[16] Si come bella sei fosti pietosa (Silvestrino)	villanesca	tenor	Dorian	G	VMABar
[17] Sospiri miei d'oime dogliorirosi et senz' aita (Adriano)	villotta	migrant*	Dorian	G	VMTBar
[18] Un giorno mi pregò una vedovella (Adriano)	villotta	tenor	Dorian	G	VMABar
[19] Vecchie letrose non valete niente (Adriano)	villanesca	migrant*	Ionian	F	VMABar
[20] Zoia zentil che per secreta via (Adriano)	canzone	tenor	Dorian	D	VSST

V = treble   T = tenor, C-clef on line 4
S = soprano, C-clef on line 1   Bar = baritone, F-clef on line 3
M = mezzo-soprano, C-clef on line 2   B = bass, F-clef on line 4
A = alto, C-clef on line 3   *The tune lies mainly in the tenor.

donists who argued that they were lascivious and demoralizing songs sung to stimulate unhealthy passions, particularly in the company of the lowest class of courtesan, the *meretrici*. Thomaso Garzoni da Bagnacavallo (1549-89) listed several kinds of secular music which he insisted were responsible for the moral turpitude prevalent among Venetian youths of his time:

> About Procurers and Procuresses: Often the ears of youths are delighted by music which softens the heart to every lasciviousness, ruins good behavior, dispels honesty, inflames the soul with burning love, and stimulates the mind to carnal desire. *Lamenti, disperationi, frottole, stanze, terzetti, canzoni, villanelle, barzelette* are sung; the lute is strummed to an amorous battle piece ... one is inadvertently invited to balls and dances where sensations go spinning, kisses become too loving, words too secret. Hands are clasped in hiding and sometimes one is led away to dark places to shameful and outrageous actions.[28]

Garzoni was no less pessimistic about the musicians who performed this music whom he charged with three vices: capricious temperament, addiction to the bottle, and a "preference for singing lascivious madrigals and empty, ridiculous Neapolitan *villanelle*."[29]

The Compositions

The majority of compositions in Willaert's collection can be identified as Neapolitan songs, which explains why the printers chose to advertise their editions under the title *Canzone villanesche alla napolitana*. However, besides fourteen *villanesche*, there are two *villotte*, one *mascherata alla napolitana*, and three *canzoni* (see Fig. 1). These four genres are differentiated in the present edition on the basis of a systematic investigation of similar pieces in sources dating from 1537 to 1550.[30] Distinctions between the genres can be made by comparing metrical forms, regional expressions, and musical styles. Sixteenth-century generic classifications are often misleading; the printers, unaware of primary stylistic differences, sometimes used the terms *villanesca* and *villotta* synonymously because of their similar rustic connotation and etymological derivation (e.g., Gardane's signature identification, "Villotte di M. Adriano").

The adjective *villanesca* is derived from the Latin noun *villanus* (Italian, *villano*; north Italian dialects, *vilàn* or *vilòte*), an individual of humble origin (see Illus. 1). The word denotes a musical-poetic style which, although presented in a written or fixed manner, draws on selected aspects of a rural, oral

ILLUS. 1. Pietro Bertelli,
Diversarum nationum habitus
(Pavia: P. Bertelli, 1594), p. 72.
(Courtesy, Biblioteca Universitaria, Bologna)

tradition for inspiration. The *villanesca* poem is normally composed of four symmetrical strophes which vary from three to eight lines in length. Northern printers and composers often reduced the number of strophes to three; they sacrificed one of the internal strophes, but retained the fourth which contains a shift in rhyme scheme essential to the structure of the poem. The strophes are created by expanding a series of four changing hendecasyllabic couplets with a refrain that varies in length. The refrain recurs unchanging in all strophes, or is modified in the final strophe to make a rhyme connection with the final rhymed couplet: (1) ab/R (2) ab/R (3) ab/R (4) cc/R. The poetic origins of the *villanesca* can be traced to a fifteenth-century repertory of popular *strambotti* in Neapolitan dialect from which it derived its characteristic pattern of changing couplets (ab ab ab cc) and its casual, colloquial tone.[31] A *villanesca* is thus a *strambotto* enlarged by the insertion of a recurrent refrain. The southern *mascherata* has the same metrical form as the *villanesca*, but differs in content. Whereas the *villanesca* is a lighthearted poem of frustrated love, the *mascherata* is a boastful serenade of a specific company

ILLUS. 2. Pietro Bertelli,
Diversarum nationum habitus
(Pavia: P. Bertelli, 1594), p. 73.
(Courtesy, Biblioteca Universitaria, Bologna)

among some Venetian aristocrats who sponsored Ruzante's troupe between 1520 and 1526. This interest continued unabated and culminated in a logical and positive response to the rustic dialect songs from Naples when they arrived in the 1540s.

Neapolitan poems were written by amateur versifiers who worked within the limits of a strophic framework because it allowed for a series of progressive expansions on a single feeling, namely, love. The poems are *centone* of short proverbial or colloquial phrases, often juxtaposed with pseudo-Petrarchan conceits, exaggerated or simplified for the sake of innocent humor or gentle caricature. The amorous protagonists of these poems are ordinary people and not necessarily peasants. Their pathetic laments convey the spirit of a simple, uncomplicated existence which the cultivated audience associated with a rural, "folkish" way of life. Stock themes and stereotyped characters and situations, for which there are counterparts in traditional Italian *strambotti* and improvised comedy, came to be permanent stylistic fixtures in these poems: the cuckolded lover who alternately praises and scolds his mistress (nos. [2], [7], [10], [11]); the frustrated swain who pleads for recognition in a nostalgic serenade (nos. [1], [6], [9], [14]); the cunning bumpkin who uses bird cries to personify his desire (nos. [5], [8]); the derisive fellow who mocks a jealous hag (*mala vecchia*), guardian of his beloved (nos. [4], [19]).

In the *villanesca* repertory there is a wide variety of musical forms, all of which are governed by the same structural principle: economical repetition of short phrases or strains marked off by cadences. The individual strophe consists of a series of well-defined strains, one for each line of text. Seven standard musical forms which developed during the 1540s for poems of three to five lines show a preference for schematic arrangements of repeated strains at the beginning and the end:

Couplet	/	Refrain		
:A:	B	:C:		
:A:	:B:	:C:		
:A:	B	:C	D:	
:A:	B	C	:D:	
:A:	B	:C:	:D:	
:A:	:B:	C	:D:	
:A:	B	:C	D	E:

In Willaert's collection most *villanesche* conform to these standard designs. Some deviate slightly with a single statement of the opening strain (nos. [1], [5], [8]). Two others, which fall in an atypical six-line

of maskers who address themselves to women of easy virtue (see Illus. 2). The braggarts identify their finest qualities—an excuse for flaunting *machismo* in blunt double meanings.

The *villotta* is a poem of one strophe which varies in length and lacks a refrain, but may contain a verse line (or lines) of nonsense syllables. Some *villotte* contain expressions in Paduan or Venetian dialect. The designation *villotta*, which originated in northern Italy ca. 1520, refers to the rustic quality of the lyrics which composers set to music in a wide variety of polyphonic styles. Ruzante, a Paduan actor and playwright (1502-42), had his traveling troupe of comedians sing *villotte* in pantomimed *mascherate* which sketched a scene of country life:

First came the buffoons, Zuan Polo and others, likewise Ruzante the Paduan, in peasant costumes who did acrobatics and danced very well, and six dressed as *vilani putati* who sang *villotte*. Each of them had various rustic items in their hands, *viz.*, hoes, shovels, spades, and rakes.[32]

A lively interest in theatrical entertainments and lyric poetry in dialect (*lingua villanescha*) developed category, resemble the madrigal in their proportions and amplification of the final line: ABCDEB'B" (no. [6]); :AB: CDEFF' (no. [15]). In the compositions with standard designs, the second line of the couplet is a transitional strain within an asymmetrical tripartite form. It functions as a short area of tonal contrast or it initiates a modulation in a narrow circle of fifths which extends into the refrain, arriving at the tonic in the final strain. Thus the form of a typical *villanesca* is articulated by a carefully planned hierarchy of cadences that bear a close relationship to the basic mode of the piece.

The earliest Neapolitan *villanesche*, such as those by Nola, are characterized by lightly flowing syllabic declamation in the cantus supported by a discreet background of sonority in the tenor and bass, which often parallels the tune in similar motion. Imitation is brief and decorative in the context of vertically oriented polyphony. The three-voice style, in which the supporting parts have little autonomy, was probably inspired by the habits of popular singers (or *citaredi*) who accompanied their lyrical recitations with simple chords on a stringed instrument. In northern Italy this essentially soloistic texture was expanded by the addition of the altus and reworked to produce a "choral" arrangement in the style of a madrigal. Techniques of *villanesca* arrangement can be studied in four compositions from Willaert's collection which have extant three-voice models:

Cingari simo	Nola-Willaert	nos. [21], [3]
Madonn'io non lo so	Nola-Willaert	nos. [22], [7]
O Dio se vede	Nola-Silvestrino	nos. [23], [10]
O dolce vita mia	Nola-Willaert	nos. [24], [11]

The arrangements vary from almost literal appropriations of the original textures (no. [10]) to more expansive elaborations. Willaert placed Nola's cantus tune in the tenor without any modification, except transposition, to accommodate the wider compass required by four voices. With the tune in this position, Willaert could derive new harmonic and contrapuntal combinations from the model. The most inventive aspect of the arrangement technique involved juxtaposing passages quoted literally from the model with reworkings of the original textures. Willaert often converted Nola's imitative textures to homophony and thereby placed the outline of the tune in sharper focus (nos. [7], [11]). In rearranging Nola's closely spaced points of imitation, Willaert created an intricate counterpoint of rhythms rather than of motives. In these recast textures, one voice was often rhythmically opposed to the other three (no. [3]).

Rhythmic independence of the parts is also a feature of some *villanesca* arrangements which lack models; a notable example is "Sempre mi ride" (no. [15]), where three different rhythmic patterns occur simultaneously in the refrain to underscore laughing syllables. Literal quotation of a vertical slice from the model occurs most frequently at phrase endings where the cantus-tenor framework of the stylized Neapolitan cadence can be easily inverted and the bass line retained. Neapolitan tunes invariably cadence with a descent by wholestep to the tonic. Typical of Pan-European repertories unaffected by polyphony, this melodic progression is by no means restricted to Neapolitan song. But the progression was regularly utilized by Neapolitan composers in the cantus parts of their polyphonic *villanesche* where, thus exposed, it was perceived as a melodic habit common to traditional Italian music. The approach to the tonic through the leading tone, on the other hand, seems to be extraneous to traditional tunes of southern Europe. Significantly, Neapolitan composers placed this progression in the inner part.

Eleven *villanesche* do not have extant polyphonic models. However, they do contain a predominant tune either in the cantus or tenor, or else a melody that can be traced as a migrating line between these two parts (see Fig. 1). Eight of them contain tunes that have stylistic elements in common with an extant corpus of *villanesche* that can be identified as Neapolitan in origin. These elements are as follows: 1) stepwise melodic descent to the tonic at cadences; 2) frequent changes of direction in the melodic line; 3) the Neapolitan trademark of truncated words and phrases. Thus, these *villanesche* (nos. [2], [4], [6], [8], [14], [15], [16], [19]) are probably arrangements of three-voice Neapolitan *villanesche* now lost. The remaining three *villanesche* ascribed to Willaert (nos. [1], [5], [9]) constitute a separate category. Their tunes are composed of shorter, more compact phrases which move in conjunct motion within a restricted range and consist mainly of minor thirds and declamatory patterns of repeated notes.[33] Thus, the pieces in this category display a higher degree of motivic unity than the aforementioned melodic types. Harmonized in strict homorhythmic textures, the tunes are highlighted by stuttering false starts, a feature developed by Nola in imitation of a southern style of singing, e.g., "O bene mio fa . . . fam'uno favore." These three compositions appear to be Willaert's "ideal" recreations of a special lyric tradition. Closely related to nos. [1], [5], and [9] in style and spirit is the homophonic *villotta* "Sospiri miei" (no. [17]). Its tune, composed of very short phrases, is shared between the cantus and tenor in a series of repeated strains (:A: :B: :CD: :ECD:).

Willaert's *canzoni* (nos. [12], [13], [20]) are settings of lyric poems by Ruzante. Gardane advertised a "Canzon di Ruzante" on the title page of his first edition of Willaert's *villanesche* (W1545Ga), but for some unknown reason it was never printed. The same promotional statement had been given by Scotto in his first edition (W1544Sc), but the present defective condition of this print precludes any definite conclusions concerning the publication of a "Canzon di Ruzante" in that year. The 1548 editions (W1548Sc and W1548Ga), however, did advertise and include the composition "Zoia zentil" which must have been popularly known as Ruzante's *Canzon*. It bears the unequivocal heading "La Canzon di Ruzante" in each part book.[34]

The three *canzoni* poems, originally multistrophic and dialectal, were reduced to one strophe and extensively edited by the composer (or printer) to appeal to a wider audience. These poems contain combinations of paired and unpaired rhyming lines in verse-lengths of odd-numbered syllables, like the free prosody of some madrigals.[35] The term "canzon" was used to identify these compositions in the *tavola* of the 1563 edition, although the expression "*villotta-madrigal*" would have served equally well to describe their musical and poetic styles.[36]

Like the *villotta* "Un giorno mi pregò una vedovella" (no. [18]), the three *canzoni* have the older mensuration sign ₵ and are based on simple, repetitive tenor tunes. "Occhio non fu" (no. [12]) and "Quando di rose" (no. [13]) are plain homophonic settings in a declamatory style. "Zoia zentil" (no. [20]) is more contrapuntal (but not imitative) and contains an animated "fa-la" section. The tenor tunes of the *canzoni* are strikingly similar which suggests that they might have been written at about the same time or derived from the same melodic tradition. Characterized by a high degree of motivic unity, the tenor tunes contain similar descending approaches to the cadence and scalar melodic figures enlivened by patterns of repeated notes. Economical use of the same melodic phrase with a different line of text is a mannerism which sets the tunes of the *canzoni* apart from the *villanesche*. A chain of repeating units is created in the tenors of "Occhio non fu" (AA'BB'CCDD) and "Zoia zentil" (AA'BBCC'DD'EFF).[37] Willaert set the lyrics with his customary sensitivity to expressive content and prosody. Such vocally conceived settings of dialectal texts contributed in large measure to the formation of the early madrigal style in

northern Italy,[38] and many would have been appropriate genre pieces in *intermedii* or improvised comedies such as those staged by Ruzante and his troupe in Venice (1520-26) and Ferrara (1529-32). *Canzoni* were also sung at social gatherings. On January 24, 1529, after the sixth course at a Ferrarese banquet, "Ruzante and five companions and two women sang very beautiful *canzoni* and madrigals in Paduan dialect."[39]

A small group of compositions in Willaert's collection are scored for equal voices (*a voci pari*) or changed voices (*a voci mutate*) in a short range of clefs, as opposed to normally spaced clefs (see Fig. 1). The cantus parts of the *villanesche* "A quand'a quand'haveva" and "O bene mio" were originally assigned the rubric "In diapason, si place," which means that the cantus could be sung an octave lower, if desired (see Plate II). The result would be a composition for contralto, two tenors, and bass in which the extremes of the outer voices would not exceed two octaves. This style of writing corresponds to Zarlino's definition of composition *a voci mutate* in *Le istitutioni harmoniche*.[40] The *canzoni*, on the other hand, were scored for high clefs and the three upper parts move in the range of a twelfth over a tenor in the manner of high-voiced compositions *a voci pari* described by Zarlino. This texture was not new to Willaert for he had composed a motet for female quartet in 1518 ("O gemma clarissima"). The *canzoni* of Willaert's series might well have been conceived for four women, although the singer on the lowest part would have to descend to d or c. Yet a similar total range (d-f") was expected of the female singers who performed Corteccia's high-voiced madrigal "Hor chi mai cantera" at the wedding of Cosimo I in 1539. The combination of high clefs is rare in Italian secular music before 1550. Besides Corteccia's madrigal, there are a few other early examples which were probably composed for specific occasions and with particular singers in mind. To this group we can tentatively add Willaert's settings of Ruzante's *canzoni* which might have been intended for the four Greek women ("le signore Greghette") employed by Alvise Cornaro of Padua, Ruzante's patron from 1532 to 1542. After Ruzante's death in 1542, Cornaro hired these women, professional singers from Venice, to entertain him in the manner to which he had been accustomed during Ruzante's tenure. In his letters the aging Cornaro describes the joyful atmosphere that pervades his Paduan villa when the women sing "with diction so perfect that all the words can be heard."[41] In a letter dated February 1551, Cornaro mentions that he has been collecting the "comedies and all the other works of the divine

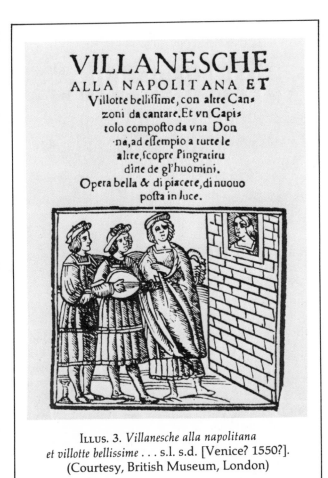

ILLUS. 3. *Villanesche alla napolitana et villotte bellissime . . . s.l. s.d. [Venice? 1550?].* (Courtesy, British Museum, London)

poet, Ruzante." It is conceivable that as part of his personal mission to revive the memory of Ruzante, Cornaro asked Willaert to set his favorite lyrics to music.

In summary, the vocal compositions in Willaert's series represent a unified corpus because they project a lighthearted tone through the use of popular tunes and texts. The corpus can, however, be divided into two broad stylistic categories which cut across the genres. Erich Hertzmann noted this division and thought it indicated a chronological pattern.[42] He took the year 1541 (when Nola's *villanesca* books were first published in Venice) as the dividing line between what he termed early and late styles, attributing the difference to Nola's influence. The so-called early compositions, which he dated ca. 1540-2, have the predominant tune in the cantus, mensuration sign ₵, and prevailing homophonic textures. The later compositions (ca. 1545) have tenor tunes, complex rhythmic patterns, contrapuntal textures, word painting, and stylized Neapolitan cadences. However, certain contradictions in this chronology present themselves as the compositions are examined. Moreover, the *terminus ante*

quem of 1540 should be viewed with caution since recent studies of other works by Willaert indicate that he did not always publish his music immediately after it was written.[43]

The commercial success of Willaert's popular songs may be partially explained by their dissemination in the medium of lute intabulation. The Venetian intabulators of Willaert's *villanesche* did not parody or gloss the compositions with excessive or difficult diminutions. Rather, by respecting the simple textures of the models, the intabulators accommodated the amateur lute player and preserved the essence of the popular style as well. Some of Abondante's intabulations of Willaert's *villanesche* are lightly decorated with passing tones, scales, and ornamented cadences (nos. [25], [28]), while others of them are completely literal adaptations (nos. [27], [29]). Pisador's arrangements for voice and vihuela, composed for a similar market in Spain, are literal intabulations with no embellishment. Lute players are often depicted with singers in woodcuts on the title pages of popular poetry books which were published regularly in small, economical editions after 1550 (see Illus. 3). The strophes of "hit tunes" from popular music repertories were printed separately from the music and probably sung to a simple chordal accompaniment from a tablature or from memory. Thus it is clear that the image of the self-accompanying popular singer, whose style inspired the earliest *villanesca* composers, made a deep and lasting impression on amateur and professional practitioners of the art.

Printing History

All the editions in Willaert's series were printed in single-impression typography in oblong quarto format.[44] The pages measure about 15 x 20 cm. (6 x 8 inches) with five or six staves to a page, an arrangement that allowed ample space for one musical composition and any additional strophes of the poem. Gerolamo Scotto and Antonio Gardane, Willaert's Venetian publishers, virtually monopolized the business of music printing in sixteenth-century Italy. They have been described as competitors who engaged in a price war which eventually led to a decline in the quality of their publications.[45] Daniel Heartz discovered, however, that the initial musical typography of both printers was identical, and he suggested that they might have been partners at an early time in their careers.[46] Measurements of some musical type faces from the prints in Willaert's series reveal that the printers did draw upon the same font of musical

Measurements of Musical Types in the Sources

	S1542Sc	W1544Sc	W1545Ga	W1548Ga	W1548Sc	W1553Ga	W1563Sc
Proportion of staff-C height to minim[47]	10/11	10/10.5	10/10.5	10/10.5	10/10.5	10/10.5	11/11
Height of double bar	13.5	13	13	13.5	13.5	13.5	14.5
Dimensions of the semibreve (w x h)	2.5 x 3.5	2.5 x 4	2.5 x 4	2.5 x 3.5	2.5 x 4	2.5 x 3.5	2.5 x 3.5
Height of the soprano clef, two vertical members	12.5/11	12.5/11	12.5/11	13/11	12.5/11	12.5/11	13/11.5

types, at least for this series, with the possible exception of W1563Sc. However, whether they purchased the types from the same source or shared them by mutual agreement is not clear. The measurements, summarized in the table above, are given in millimeters (variations in size of .5 mm. can be attributed to paper shrinkage).

A comparative study of typographical detail made with the aid of photocopies showed that not only were the same musical types and initials used for each edition, but also that the type was newly set each time. Thus, the compositors worked with a limited stock of types as was often the case in the hand-press period in small shops.[48] Each book is distinguished by its compositor's mannerisms regarding note-spacing, text underlay, placement, and choice of initials. With each successive edition, musical and textual emendations were made; the most substantive changes occur at the beginning of the series. Thus, Willaert probably did not personally supervise the editing after 1545; the firms were probably large enough by this time to employ correctors. Gardane's business was relatively new, having been established in 1538.[49] The Scotto family, on the other hand, had run a flourishing enterprise in Venice since 1479. Gerolamo Scotto was granted his first printing privilege in 1536, but he did not print with musical types until 1539 at which time he worked independently from other music printers in the family, Brandino and Ottaviano (IV) Scotto. At the beginning of his printing career, Gerolamo Scotto probably did not operate with any stronger financial security than Gardane. Between 1535 and ca. 1547 the family capital was concentrated in the shop of Ottaviano (II) Scotto, Gerolamo's brother and heir of Amadio Scotto, head of the firm from 1499 to 1535. Gerolamo finally did inherit this prosperous branch of the firm at Ottaviano's death, ca. 1547.[50]

Gerolamo Scotto and Gardane may have had to share materials during the 1540s so they could put out enough books to realize a profit. Expenses and labor costs could be reduced by the simultaneous shared setting of types which, if necessary, was done in different shops. Compositors formed companionships for the efficient and equitable distribution of labor, a process that was facilitated by the casting-off technique and setting by formes.[51] Casting-off allowed the overseer to determine accurately the exact content of each page. Typesetting could then begin anywhere in the book and more than one part could be set at a time. Several pages could be arranged in a "forme" on one large sheet, allowing a compositor to set all the pages for one side of a given sheet and then send them to be printed before the pages for the other side were set. This procedure made a limited stock of type go further. However, since the processes of book production are so involved, it is seldom possible to deduce from evidence in any one book how it was set and printed. Thus it cannot be determined to what extent Scotto and Gardane might . have cooperated for Willaert's series, if at all. Yet there is one source that suggests they might have worked together for a time during the 1540s. In the *Primo libro de madrigali italiani . . . a due voci* by Jhan Gero, printed by Gardane in 1541, Scotto signed the dedication which he wrote to Cesare Visconti on behalf of "casa nostra."[52]

By 1546 Gardane had earned a brilliant reputation for his contributions to the musical life of Venice. In that year the poet Gerolamo Fenaruolo celebrated Gardane's stellar achievements in the sonnet translated below:

In the hour when the sun is only
A faint glimmering of itself,
Your star, Gardane, ascends
With such splendor
That it moves us to sing. . . .
For Parabosco, Cambio and Rore
You have brought forth sweet words and songs. . . .
I know of no one who would refuse

To be admitted to your circle
And who would not turn toward heaven and
  plead:
Stars, light my way to the magnificent press
And grant me rest at San Zacharia.[53]

Gardane attained a high level of technical perfection in the single-impression method. He was more successful than Scotto in obtaining horizontal continuity with staff segments, almost eliminating the spaces between them. An anonymous visitor to Venice paid tribute to Gardane's articulate products in the following terms:

> Of the music books that I saw in Venice there were those by the Venetian, Gardane, neatly printed and decorated with every precaution taken in the impression. Madrigals, *canzoni*, and *villanelle* are sung in Venice now that Gardane has given them public recognition.[54]

However, Scotto should receive the credit for discovering and promoting the new popular style that was destined to rival the madrigal in Venice during the 1540s and 1550s, since he was responsible for the first editions of *villanesche* by Nola and Willaert. Having initiated Willaert's series in 1544, he also brought the cycle to an end with a posthumous anthology of madrigals and *napolitane* in 1563. In 1542, the year of Willaert's first trip to Flanders, Scotto included two *villanesche a voci pari* in a volume of his own madrigals (S1542Sc), which are the only known *villanesche* printed between 1541 (N1541Sc) and 1544. Moreover, they are the only extant examples with the additional strophes of the poem printed between the staves rather than in a group at the bottom of the page (see Plate II). Only a fragment of W1544Sc has survived, the first gathering (four leaves) of a foliated altus part book with title page.[55] W1563Sc is also incomplete, lacking the altus part book. Scotto may have used portions of S1542Sc and W1544Sc as copy text for the posthumous edition, or even the composer's manuscript which he could have retained over the years. The cantus rubric "In diapason, si placet" with the *villanesche* in S1542Sc was repeated in W1563Sc, and probably also in W1544Sc, but it does not appear in the intervening editions. Moreover, many editorial corrections in W1548Sc, W1548Ga, and W1553Ga, which form a simple ancestral group within the series (i.e., the books can all be traced to the same copy text), were not carried over into W1563Sc.

W1545Ga stands apart from the other editions in appearance and arrangement. Using a very small italic letter type, Gardane printed additional strophes for many of the poems, whereas Scotto

had given only the first strophe of each multi-strophic *villanesca* in 1544. W1545Ga was definitely not the copy text for the 1548 editions because the line-by-line distribution of material on the staves is quite different. A new internal arrangement was needed for these editions because four pieces from W1545Ga were dropped and two others added (see Fig. 2). W1548Ga and W1548Sc are identical in contents and the order in which pieces appear, but differ in small typographical details. Neither print contains a dedication, so we do not know which came out first. One edition was clearly used as copy text for the other, because the words and music are distributed on the staves in exactly the same manner. Scotto used the same italic type for text underlay and additional strophes, while Gardane preferred a larger italic with decorative swash capitals for the strophes (see also W1553Ga). The contents and order of compositions in W1553Ga are derived from W1548Ga, which probably served as copy text. The line-by-line disposition of material on the staves is identical in seven pieces and very similar in the remaining seven.

Editorial Method: Vocal Compositions

The present edition attempts to represent the composers' original intentions as closely as possible. The vocal compositions have been transcribed from the earliest-known editions to have survived in complete form on the assumption that each successive edition contains a higher percentage of "accidental" alterations made by the printer or his corrector. For this repertory the second edition is the central source for most compositions, the first edition being incomplete, defective, or lost. Second editions have a certain degree of authority because they are apt to contain the composers' own "substantive" corrections of printing errors in the first edition. That W1544Sc is defective is unfortunate, for according to the title page the proofs were read by Willaert himself ("da lui diligentemente corretti"). However, W1545Ga serves very well as the central source for the majority of compositions because it has survived in excellent condition (see Plate I).

Variants between the central source and other editions are tabulated in the Critical Notes. Musical variants and printing errors can be traced from the Critical Notes to the scores by a system of measure and voice-part designation. Textual variants are noted on the poems, which are printed separately in the Critical Notes so that the structure of the poem can be clearly understood. The compositions have been transcribed at original pitch in a 2:1 re-

Figure 2. Distribution of Compositions in Willaert's Series*

Incipit	S1542Sc	W1544Sc	W1545Ga	W1548Ga	W1548Sc	W1553Ga	W1563Sc
[1] A quand'a quand'haveva una vicina (Adriano)	x	x	x	x	x	x	x
[2] Buccucia dolce chiù che canamielle (Piersson)				x	x	x	
[3] Cingari simo venit'a giocare (Adriano)		x	x	x	x	x	x
[4] Le vecchie per invidia sono pazze (Corteccia)		[x]	x	x	x	x	
[5] Madonna mia famme bon'offerta (Adriano)		x	x	x	x	x	x
[6] Madonna mia io son un poverello (Anon.)		[x]	x				
[7] Madonn'io non lo so perchè lo fai (Adriano)		x	x	x	x	x	x
[8] Madonn'io t'haggi amat'et amo assai (Corteccia)		[x]	x				
[9] O bene mio fam'uno favore (Adriano)	x	[x]	x	x	x	x	x
[10] O Dio si vede chiaro cha per te moro (Silvestrino)			x	x	x	x	
[11] O dolce vita mia che t'haggio fatto (Adriano)		[x]	x	x	x	x	
[12] Occhio non fu giamai che lachrimasse (Adriano)		[x]					x
[13] Quando di rose d'oro (Adriano)		[x]					x
[14] Se mille volte ti vengh'a vedere (Silvestrino)			x				
[15] Sempre mi ride sta donna da bene (Adriano)		[x]	x	x	x	x	
[16] Si come bella sei fosti pietosa (Silvestrino)			x				
[17] Sospiri miei d'oime dogliorirosi et senz'aita (Adriano)		[x]	x	x	x	x	
[18] Un giorno mi pregò una vedovella (Adriano)		x	x	x	x	x	
[19] Vecchie letrose non valete niente (Adriano)		x	x	x	x	x	
[20] Zoia zentil che per secreta via (Adriano)		[x]		x	x	x	x
	2	[16]	16	14	14	14	8

*S1542Sc is not properly a part of the series, but its two *villanesche* have been listed here to complete the chronology. The contents of W1544Sc (a defective print of which only a fragment survives) has been reconstructed according to information given on the title page of the print. See also fn. 55.

duction. The incipit of each part includes the original clef, mensuration sign, a modern symbol to represent the value of the original initial note (omitting any rests), and the range.

Bar lines

The popular songs by Willaert and his circle are word-oriented compositions characterized by a close alliance between the rhythmic accents of the "speaking line" and the "singing line." In order to emphasize this basic feature of the popular style, the editor has adopted a method of accentual barring with changing time signatures. Editorial bar lines mark off measures containing conventional patterns of strong and weak beats which are arranged to coincide with stressed and unstressed syllables in the poetry. This disposition of bar lines is intended to increase the performer's understanding of the basic compositional process, encourage a sensitive response to textual prosody, and aid in pronunciation.

A typical hendecasyllabic line of Italian verse contains a pattern of accents in varying strengths and in asymmetrical positions. The principal accent (*suono temperato*) falls on the penultimate syllable, while a secondary stress can occur on the sixth, or more rarely on the fourth syllable. In setting these lines to music, composers aimed to match the stressed syllables of the poem with long rhythmic values and unstressed syllables with short ones.[56] A stressed syllable can be underscored by a rhythmic value that is longer in relation to those around it and the syllable can be further emphasized by a strong harmonic progression or by a rest that interrupts the progress of the phrase. Syllables without accent are treated as connectives between stresses and have shorter rhythmic values and weaker harmonic progressions. The following examples illustrate the normal distribution of text accents and some common musical solutions in this repertory:

The insertion of editorial bar lines is determined by reflections of text accent in those voices which form the structural framework of the composition

(the part which carries the tune) and the bass, which provides harmonic support. The most natural correlation of textual and musical accents is found in the tune. Whether exposed in the uppermost part or hidden in the tenor, the accentual design of the melody part is clarified by the harmonic rhythm generated by the bass. Even if the other parts oppose the tune with cross accents, the tune normally maintains a stable relationship to the bass.

When bar lines are distributed according to text accents, a principal ingredient of the stylistic language, namely, the inevitable feminine cadences at phrase endings, is clarified. In the feminine cadence the principal accent on the penultimate syllable is underscored by dominant harmony (see example) and a syncopated dissonance. The resolution on the tonic chord always coincides with an unaccented syllable and is thus relegated to the weaker position. The essential stress patterns governing the feminine cadence are communicated most precisely in short measures which have clearly defined positions for strong and weak beats, e.g., the 2/4 and 3/4 measures. In this edition most feminine cadences are located in one of these temporal units. Since the choice of measure is conditioned by the value of the final syllable and the activity of the succeeding phrase, it is occasionally convenient to use the 4/4 measure.

The final chord of each composition always has the value of a *longa* (signified here by a fermata) in the sources. The duration of the final chord was customarily left to the discretion of the performers. The value of the *longa* has been reinterpreted in this edition in order to complete the cadential patterns in a balanced manner, because the final chord should be precisely measured for the sake of a smooth transition if another strophe follows. Its ultimate value can be sung as given or extended *ad libitum*.

Accidentals

The composers' signs for chromatic alteration printed in the source are placed immediately before the notes to which they apply. Editorial accidentals (*musica ficta*) are added above the pitches to which they apply and are valid only for the note so marked. Cautionary accidentals given in parentheses on the staff remind the performer to observe a cross relation or to cancel an accidental which should not be carried through a measure (the duration of accidentals is ambiguous in the sources). Editorial solutions should be viewed as informed suggestions. Because sixteenth-century theorists and composers often applied the same rules in different ways, performers should have the option to accept, modify, or reject the alternatives offered here. Practical evidence for differing approaches to half-step inflection can be found in the intabulations of Willaert's *villanesche*. The intabulators often modified some of the composer's original inflections or added new ones. The editor has not intentionally altered a vocal composition to conform to its intabulation, since both composition and intabulation represent valid practices in the mid-sixteenth century.

Gioseffo Zarlino, Willaert's celebrated disciple, said that "the semitone is truly the salt, the seasoning, and the cause of every good melody and harmony."[57] This basic axiom summarizes the harmonic language, based on a modality enriched by the liberal use of accidentals, used by the Venetian circle around Willaert. Moreover, the accidentals are often precisely indicated in the score. For example, these composers frequently heightened the unity of a phrase in transposed Dorian on g by adding e-flat throughout the phrase anticipating the cadence. Generally the composers followed, in written practice, the "fa-la" rule of *musica ficta* which required that the single note above *la* should be solmized *fa* and flattened if the interval is not already a semitone. In some situations where they might have supplied b-flat or e-flat but did not, the editor has added accidentals according to principles consistent with the practice of the Venetian composers, e.g., they often flattened *fa* where *la* is either preceded or quitted by a leap of a third. These composers seldom notated the raised leading tone, probably because the *subsemitonium modi* rule of *musica ficta* was widely practiced at the time. According to Stefano Vanneo, "sharps for the *subsemitonium* in cadences should be written exclusively for beginners who want everything spelled out."[58] Silvestrino added sharps more consistently than the other composers in order to create major triads and to expedite modulation in a wider circle of fifths. He may have felt the influence of Nicola Vicentino who was preoccupied with the practical use of the chromatic genera in the 1540s.[59] Vicentino said that accidentals can change the nature of a composition: "flats tend to make a piece melancholy and if the composer wants a happy effect he should use animated steps, especially the major third in fast motion" (*L'antica musica ridotta alla moderna prattica*, 1555).[60]

Mensuration Signs

The majority of *villanesche* in this collection have the mensuration sign C (*misura di breve*). The note values are short with much of the text declaimed in minims or semiminims (*note nere*) in contrast to the prevailing white notes of the compositions in ₵ (*misura commune*). In the *Lucidario* (1545), Pietro Aron stated that a breve in ₵ and a semibreve in C are the same thing, which is to say that pieces in ₵ and C are merely graphic variants of the same musical style.[61] According to Glareanus there is no fixed proportional relationship between C and ₵ when these signs are used for entire pieces but "₵ is a sign that can be used if one wants to accelerate the tactus a bit."[62] Editorial tempo markings do not appear in the transcriptions, but performers should follow the advice of Vicentino who said that "*vilotte* and *napolitane* demand a fast tempo from the start."[63] In general the tactus or unit of time beating should fall on the semibreve (half-note) for compositions in ₵. For some compositions in C the semibreve might be taken as the unit of measure as suggested by Vicentino.[64] For others the minim would be a better choice, as advocated by Thomaso Cimello, a Neapolitan composer, theorist, and contemporary of Nola.[65] The choice of tactus is determined by the prevailing time-unit of the composition. A sixteenth-century performance practice noted by Vicentino may be helpful to interpreters of this style. He said, "singers may change tempo when the music calls for it, and that those who say one ought not to change tempo in beating time *alla breve*, do it nonetheless in practice."[66]

Four compositions contain contrasting passages or sections in sesquialtera proportion. Triple meter is indicated by the mensuration sign ₵3 signifying sesquialtera of the semibreve (no. [18]), by the proportion 3 within a passage in C signifying sesquialtera of the minim (no. [14]), and by the proportion 3 with coloration (no. [10] and its model, no. [23]). In the latter, the numeral 3 "annotates" the coloration. In the transcriptions the proportions are indicated by a sign of equivalence. The first value in the equation refers to *integer valor* and the second to the proportion. Coloration is indicated by small brackets ⌐ ¬.

Texts

In the past, modern editors of *villanesche* have underlaid the first strophe of text to the music and, like the early printers, have arranged the remaining strophes under the composition. However, these strophes are difficult to sing without advance decisions in regard to text underlay and vowel elision which, in many cases, requires extensive adjustments in the given material. In this edition, all the given text is underlaid below the notes following basic precepts formulated by Vicentino and Zarlino, both of which give an accurate account of Venetian practice.[67]

The poems have been left for the most part in their original state. Accents and apostrophes not given in the sources have been added when needed to clarify the meaning. Grammatical errors are an integral part of the colloquial style and therefore have not been corrected. Moreover, no attempt has been made to normalize the various spellings of dialect words since they may be of interest to philologists and linguists. A distinction exists between the southern poets who exaggerated the Neapolitan qualities of their verses with local proverbs and dialectal verb forms, and northern arrangers or editors who sought to retain enough of the southern flavor to be in vogue, yet filtered out or altered words which could not be easily understood in their region. The small but telling revisions or vestiges of the southern vocabulary are annotated in the Critical Notes. Translations of the poems may also be found in the Critical Notes. In an effort to preserve the rough, anti-literary qualities of the poetry, the translators have preferred literal, colloquial prose to polished rhymed verse.

Very few punctuation marks appear in the sources. Consequently, such marks have been added sparingly to the poems given separately in the Critical Notes and Translations. Periods suffice to indicate complete sentences. In the transcriptions, however, commas have been inserted in the text for the sole purpose of marking off partial or complete reiterations of verse lines. The translations have been fully punctuated and the reader is advised to consult them for a more complete understanding of the syntax of the poem. If a repetition was indicated by *ij* in the source, the text is editorially supplied in brackets. Words are hyphenated according to the conventional rules of syllabification for the Italian language. Additional hyphens are added when an internal syllable is sung to more than one note or tied across the bar line. An unbroken line is used in similar situations for final syllables or monosyllabic words. An ellipsis distinguishes words which are deliberately truncated in the Neapolitan style.

Editorial Method: Instrumental Compositions

The lute and vihuela transcriptions have been complemented by the addition of the original tablature on a parallel staff, according to the recommendation of the 1957 Colloquium on the lute sponsored by the Centre national de la recherche scientifique.[68] The tablature is printed exactly as it appears in the source. Brackets enclose those notes that have been changed to correct pitch errors in the tablature or added to correct omissions. Errors in the tablature's rhythmic signs are signified by asterisks placed between the tablature and the transcription. Therefore, the performer who plays from tablature must consult the transcription for the solution of errors. Support for most editorial emendations can be found in the vocal models.

The transcriptions follow the interpretive approach, i.e., the polyphonic voices are realized by the direction of note stems and the use of rests. This transcription method facilitates comparison with the vocal models as does the use of G tuning which produces the same mode as the model (except no. [32]). Irregular barring and the 2:1 reduction are retained for the sake of easy comparison (note, however, no. [26] where a 4:1 reduction is necessary to produce the values of the model). Both the Italian and Spanish tablatures contain symbols which should be clarified for the performer who plays from tablature. The dots given with certain ciphers indicate fingerings for the right hand. One dot means that the index finger (or fingers) shall be used and not the thumb. Ciphers lacking dots are played with the thumb (on the lowest string) and fingers. If the third or fourth finger should be used, then two or three dots, respectively, are given.[69] The double cross which appears in Bianchini's lute book refers to legato playing and means that the respective note or chord should sound "for the duration of a semibreve or at least as long as possible."[70] The curved *raya* above the verticals in Pisador's book signifies the transfer of the rhythmic value of a dot to the following *compás* (unit between two verticals).[71]

Acknowledgments

I wish to express my gratitude to the University of Minnesota Graduate School for a research grant in the summer of 1973 and a Putnam Dana McMillan award in the summer of 1974, which made available both the time and the funds needed for the completion of this edition. Permission to consult the sources was granted by the Archivio Capitolare in Pistoia (W1544Sc), the Bayerische Staatsbibliothek in Munich (W1545Ga, N1545Ga), the Bibliothèque Royale Albert Ier in Brussels (S1542Sc, W1563Sc), the British Museum in London (B1546Ga, P1552Pi), the Civico Museo Bibliografico Musicale in Bologna (W1548Ga), the Herzog-August-Bibliothek in Wolfenbüttel (W1545Ga, W1553Ga), and the Nationalbibliothek in Vienna (S1542Sc, W1545Ga, A1548Sc, W1548Sc). I should like to recognize the valuable contributions of friends and colleagues who generously shared their knowledge in various related fields: Theodolinda Barolini of Columbia University and Josephine

Mangano of the University of Minnesota who assisted with the translations; Vernon Hamberg who copied and proofread the transcriptions; Paul Fetler, James Haar, and Gary Hoiseth who helped solve difficult problems. Finally I owe a particular debt of gratitude to Nino Pirrotta for his keen insights regarding barring methods and linguistic problems, and for his constant help and encouragement since the inception of this project.

May 1978

Donna G. Cardamone
University of Minnesota

Notes

1. Edward Lowinsky, "A Treatise on Text Underlay by a German Disciple of Francisco de Salinas," *Festschrift Heinrich Besseler zum sechzigsten Geburtstag* (Leipzig, 1961), p. 248.

2. Gioseffo Zarlino, *Istitutioni harmoniche* (Venice: Francesco dei Franceschi, 1573), Proemio, p. 2.

3. For detailed biographical information on Nola after 1563, see Lionello Cammarota, ed., *Gian Domenico del Giovane da Nola: I documenti biografici e l'attività presso la SS. Annunziata con l'opera completa* (Rome, 1973), I:26-45. See also Donna G. Cardamone, "The Debut of the *Canzone villanesca alla napolitana*," *Studi Musicali* 4 (1975):85-96.

4. Venice, Archivio di Stato, Senato Terra, Reg. 33, c. 116, 5 IX 1544. Scotto's 1544 edition of Corteccia's second book of madrigals for four voices is not extant; it was reprinted by Gardane in 1547.

5. Giuseppe Turrini, "L'Accademia Filarmonica di Verona dalla fondazione (maggio 1543) al 1600 e il suo patrimonio musicale antico," *Atti e Memorie della Accademia di Agricoltura, Scienze e Lettere di Verona* 18 (Verona, 1941):37. The same item is listed on p. 89 from an inventory dated 1562.

6. Mario Fabri, "La vita e l'ignota opera prima di Francesco Corteccia musicista italiano del rinascimento," *Chigiana* 22 (1965):202. For a selection of Corteccia's sacred works, see Francesco Corteccia, *Eleven Works to Latin Texts*, Ann McKinley, ed., RECENT RESEARCHES IN THE MUSIC OF THE RENAISSANCE, vol. VI (Madison, Wisconsin: A-R Editions, Inc., 1969).

7. Fabri, "La vita," pp. 185-217.

8. James Haar, "Notes on the *Dialogo della musica* of Antonfrancesco Doni," *Music and Letters* 47 (1966):206.

9. G. Francesco Malipiero, ed., *Dialogo della musica*, Collana di musiche veneziane inedite e rare (Vienna, 1965), 7:281.

10. Alfred Einstein, *The Italian Madrigal* (Princeton, 1949), p. 439. For further information on Perissone as a madrigal composer see pp. 440-4.

11. Malipiero, ed., *Dialogo della musica*, p. 281.

12. Orazio Toscanella, Dedication to *I nomi antichi e moderni delle province, regioni, città & isole dell'Europa* . . . (Venice: F. Franceschini, 1567). For a translation of the dedication addressed to Antonio Zantani, which describes his circle of musicians, see Einstein, *The Italian Madrigal*, pp. 446-7.

13. "Sol fu per grazia un tempo a noi concesso, Sì raro spirto eletto e pellegrino. . . . Quando equal cambio in cambio a noi fia dato Di sì gran cambio?" Quoted by Remo Giazotto, *Harmonici concenti in aere veneto* (Rome, 1954), p. 37 from *Rime di Mons. Girolamo Fenaruolo* (Venice: Giorgio Angelieri, 1574).

14. "In un punto perì suon sì pregiato, E 'n sua vece mando tristi lamenti (duro cambio) il mar d'Adria in ogni lato." Quoted by Giazotto, *Harmonici*.

15. Gianluigi Dardo, "Abondante," *Die Musik in Geschichte und Gegenwart* (Cassel, 1949-51), I:cols. 12-13.

16. Dedication to *I nomi antichi e moderni*; see footnote 12.

17. Malipiero, ed., *Dialogo della musica*, p. 281; Vittorio Rossi, ed., *Lettere di A. Calmo* (Turin, 1888), p. 295.

18. R. de Morcourt, "Le livre de tablature de luth de Domenico Bianchini (1546)," *La musique instrumentale de la Renaissance*, ed. Jean Jacquot (Paris, 1955), pp. 186-7.

19. John M. Ward, "Pisador," *Die Musik in Geschichte und Gegenwart* (Cassel, 1962), X:cols. 1297-8.

20. For further information on the role of music in Venetian social life see Armen Carapetyan, "The *Musica Nova* of Adrian Willaert with a Reference to the Humanistic Society of 16th-Century Venice" (Ph.D. diss., Harvard University, 1945), pp. 78-91.

21. Turrini, "L'Accademia Filarmonica," p. 184.

22. Alessandro Piccolomini, *De la institutione di tutta la vita de l'homo nato nobile e in città libera* (Venice: G. Scotto, 1542), Book III, Chap. 10, fol. 50v.

23. Einstein, *The Italian Madrigal*, pp. 198-9.

24. Lowinsky, "A Treatise on Text Underlay," pp. 245-9.

25. Quoted by Giazotto, *Harmonici concenti*, p. 19.

26. Celio Malespini, *Ducento novelle . . . nelle quali si raccontano diversi avvenimenti così lieti, come mesti & stravaganti* (Venice: Al Segno dell'Italia, 1609), Part I, novella 60, fol. 169.

27. Translated by Henry Kaufmann from *L'antica musica ridotta alla moderna prattica* (Rome: A. Barré, 1555), Book IV, Chap. 26, fol. 84v, in his *The Life and Works of Nicola Vicentino*, Musicological Studies and Documents, 11 (Rome, 1966), p. 39.

28. Thomaso Garzoni, *La piazza universale di tutte le professioni del mondo* (Venice: Gio. Battista Somasco, 1589), Discorso 75, p. 607.

29. Garzoni, Discorso 62, pp. 442-3.

30. Donna G. Cardamone, "The *Canzone villanesca alla napolitana* and Related Italian Vocal Part-Music: 1537 to 1570" (Ph.D. diss., Harvard University, 1972), pp. 147-206, and "Forme metriche e musicali della canzone villanesca e della villanella alla napolitana," *Rivista Italiana di Musicologia* 12 (1977), 25-72.

31. Cardamone, "Forme metriche," pp. 25-38.

32. Marin Sanudo, *I diarii*, ed. Rinaldo Fulin *et al.* (Venice, 1890), XXXV:col. 393 (from an account dated February 4, 1524).

33. For an analysis of no. [9], "O bene mio," see Erich Hertzmann, *Adrian Willaert in der weltlichen Vokalmusik seiner Zeit*, Sammlung musikwissenschaftlicher Einzeldarstellungen, 15 (Leipzig, 1931), pp. 70-1, 85, and Wolfgang Osthoff, *Theatergesang und darstellende Musik in der italienischen Renaissance*, Münchner Veröffentlichungen zur Musikgeschichte, 14 (Tutzing, 1969), pp. 282-3.

34. In cataloging W1545Ga, Emil Vogel, *Bibliothek der gedruckten weltlichen Vokalmusik Italiens*, II: 348, added the rubric "Canzon di Ruzante" to the second piece, "O dolce vita mia," even though it was not given in the print. He followed the example of Robert Eitner, "Adrian Willaert," *Monatshefte für Musikgeschichte von der Gesellschaft für Musikforschung* 19 (1887):101, who claimed that "Zoia zentil," the second piece in W1548Sc, had to be a substitution for another piece by Ruzante. Emilio Lovarini, "Una poesia musicata del Ruzante," *Miscellanea di studi critici in onore di Vincenzo Crescini* (Cividale, 1929), p. 256, argued that if "O dolce vita mia" had been written by Ruzante, it would have been removed from W1548Sc to make space for "Zoia zentil." It was retained, however, and shifted to fifth place. "O dolce vita mia" could never have been written by Ruzante for it is distinctly Neapolitan in metrical structure and tone. It originated in the south where it was first set to music by Nola (N1541Ga).

35. Don Harrán, "Verse Types in the Early Madrigal," *Journal of the American Musicological Society* 22 (1969):36-41.

36. The term *canzone* was employed for the several kinds of *poesia per musica* in music prints of the 1520s as well as in literary anthologies throughout the century.

37. For an analysis of "Zoia zentil," see Hertzmann, *Adrian Willaert*, pp. 59-60, 84-5 and Osthoff, *Theatergesang*, pp. 240-1.

38. Walter H. Rubsamen, "From Frottola to Madrigal: The Changing Pattern of Secular Italian Vocal Music," *Chanson and Madrigal, 1480-1530*, ed. James Haar (Cambridge, Mass., 1964), pp. 51-87.

39. Cristoforo di Messisbugo, *Banchetti, compositioni di vivande et apparecchio generale* (Ferrara: Giovanni de Buglhat and Antonio Hucher, 1549), fol. B⁷.

40. Gioseffo Zarlino, *Le istitutioni harmoniche* (1558 ed.), Part III, Chap. 65.

41. The letters are printed by Alfred Mortier, *Ruzante* (Paris, 1925), pp. 235-41.

42. Hertzmann, *Adrian Willaert*, pp. 69-75, 81.

43. Lowinsky, "A Treatise on Text Underlay," pp. 245-9; James Haar, "A Diatonic Duo by Willaert," *Tijdschrift van de Vereniging voor Nederlandse Muziekgeschiedenis* 21 (1969):70; Anthony A. Newcomb, "Editions of Willaert's *Musica Nova*: New Evidence, New Speculations," *Journal of the American Musicological Society* 26 (1973):132-45; Lawrence F. Bernstein, "La Courone et fleur des chansons a troys: A Mirror of the French Chanson in Italy in the Years Between Ottaviano Petrucci and Antonio Gardane," *Journal of the American Musicological Society* 26 (1973):1-68.

44. The first print in which the single-impression method was used for vocal music in Italy is also the earliest-known collection of *villanesche*: *Canzone villanesche alla napolitana novamente stampate, libro primo* (Naples: Johannes de Colonia, 1537). For further information see Cardamone, "The Debut of the *Canzone villanesca*," pp. 76-9.

45. Claudio Sartori, "Scotto," *Die Musik in Geschichte und Gegenwart* (Cassel, 1965), XII:cols. 436-7.

46. Daniel Heartz, *Pierre Attaingnant, Royal Printer of Music* (Berkeley, 1969), p. 159.

47. For data pertinent to the proportion of staff-height to minim drawn from a wide sampling of printers' types, see Daniel Heartz, "Typography and Format in Early Music Printing," *Notes* 15 (1967):704 ff.

48. Philip Gaskell, *A New Introduction to Bibliography* (Oxford, 1972), p. 41.

49. Horatio F. Brown, *The Venetian Printing Press* (London, 1891), p. 108; Claudio Sartori, "Una dinastia di editori musicali," *La Bibliofilia* 58 (1956):176-208.

50. Claudio Sartori, "La famiglia degli Scotto," *Acta musicologica* 36 (1964):25 ff.

51. Gaskell, *A New Introduction to Bibliography*, pp. 40-3.

52. James Haar, "The *Note Nere* Madrigal," *Journal of the American Musicological Society* 18 (1965):35.

53. Quoted by Giazotto, *Harmonici concenti*, pp. 9-10 from Fenaruolo, *Nuove rime* (1546).

54. Giazotto, *Harmonici concenti*, p. 14, quoted from *Dissertazioni su i libri stampati* (Milan, Biblioteca Ambrosiana, MS. R.76 inf).

55. The contents of W1544Sc have been reconstructed in Fig. 2 to produce a hypothetical total of sixteen compositions on seven leaves (the eighth leaf would be the title page with blank verso). The shorter pieces could have been arranged two to a page, which was the case in subsequent editions. Since the title page mentioned the inclusion of some madrigals, it has been assumed, for purposes of reconstruction, that Scotto was referring to the *canzoni*.

56. One sixteenth-century theorist, Giovanni del Lago, formulated a rule ca. 1540 unique to his writings alone, which tells precisely how to coordinate musical rhythms with the natural stresses of the poetry. "In the vernacular, all verses of seven syllables have the next-to-last syllable sustained . . . and all those of eleven syllables the sixth—or sometimes the fourth, though this happens but rarely—and next-to-last syllables. But when it does happen that the fourth syllable is sustained, do not sustain the sixth, but rather the fourth and next-to-last syllables." Translated by Don Harrán, "The Theorist Giovanni del Lago: A New View of the Man and His Writings," *Musica Disciplina* 27 (1973):119.

57. Gioseffo Zarlino, *The Art of Counterpoint, Part III of Le istitutioni harmoniche* (1558), trans. Guy A. Marco and Claude V. Palisca (New Haven, 1968), p. 23.

58. Stefano Vanneo, *Recanetum de musica aurea* (Rome: Valerio Dorico, 1533), Book III, Chap. 36, p. 90.

59. Kaufmann, *The Life and Works of Nicola Vicentino*, p. 18.

60. Kaufmann, *The Life and Works of Nicola Vicentino*, pp. 154-155.

61. James Haar, "The *Note Nere* Madrigal," p. 23.

62. Glareanus, *Dodechachordon* (Basel, 1547), Book III, Chap. 8, translated by Haar, "The *Note Nere* Madrigal," pp. 24-5.

63. Kaufmann, *The Life and Works of Nicola Vicentino*, p. 151.

64. Kaufmann, *The Life and Works of Nicola Vicentino*, p. 194.

65. Thomaso Cimello, "Regole nove" (ca. 1545), Naples, Biblioteca Nazionale, VH 210, fol. 88v.

66. James Haar, "The *Note Nere* Madrigal," p. 27.

67. Don Harrán, "Vicentino and His Rules of Text Underlay," *The Musical Quarterly* 59 (1973):620-32; "New Light on the Question of Text Underlay Prior to Zarlino," *Acta musicologica* 45 (1973):32-46; Nicola Vicentino, *L'antica musica ridotta alla moderna prattica* (Rome: A. Barre, 1555); Zarlino, *Le istitutioni harmoniche*, Part IV, Chap. 33.

68. "Problèmes d'édition," *La luth et sa musique*, ed. Jean Jacquot (Paris, 1958), p. 303.

69. Daniel Heartz, "Les premières instructions pour le luth," *Le luth et sa musique*, p. 83.

70. Heartz, "Les premières instructions," p. 81, quoted from Joan Maria da Crema, *Intabolatura di lauto libro terzo* (Venice, 1546), "Regola alli lettori."

71. Thomas F. Heck, rev. of *Luis de Milan, El Maestro*, ed. Charles Jacobs, *Journal of the American Musicological Society* 25 (1972):488.

Key to Abbreviations

Printed Sources of the Music

N1541Sc *Canzoni villanesche de Don Ioan Dominico del Giovane de Nola. Libro primo et secondo. Novamente stampati.* Venice: Scotto, 1541 (C,T,B). This source was destroyed during World War II. It was in a collection sold to the Preussische Staatsbibliothek, Berlin, in 1909 by the Kirchen-Ministerial-Bibliothek, Celle.

S1542Sc *Madrigali a quatro voce di Geronimo Scotto con alcuni a la misura breve, et altri a voce pari novamente posti in luce. Libro primo.* Venice: Scotto, 1542 (C,A,T,B).

W1544Sc *Canzone villanesche alla napolitana di M. Adriano Wigliaret a quatro voci, con alcuni madrigali da lui nuovamente composti & diligentemente corretti, con la canzona di Ruzante. Con la giunta di alcune altre canzone villanesche alla napolitana a quatro voci, composte da M. Francesco Corteccia non piu viste ne stampate, nuovamente poste in luce.* Venice: Scotto, 1544 (A, fragment).

W1545Ga *Canzone villanesche alla napolitana di M. Adriano Wigliaret a quatro voci con la canzona di Ruzante. Con la gionta di alcune canzone villanesche alla napolitana di Francesco Silvestrino ditto Chechin et di Francesco Corteccia novamente stampate con le soe stanze. Primo libro a quatro voci.* Venice: Gardane, 1545 (C,A,T,B).

N1545/1Ga *Canzone villanesche de Don Ioan Domenico del Giovane de Nola, a tre voci novamente ristampate. Libro primo.* Venice: Gardane, 1545 (C,T,B).

N1545/2Ga *Canzone villanesche de Don Ioan Domenico del Giovane de Nola, a tre voci novamente ristampate. Libro secundo.* Venice: Gardane, 1545 (C,T,B).

B1546Ga *Intabolatura de lauto di Dominico Bianchini ditto Rossetto di recercari motetti madrigali canzon francese napolitane et balli novamente stampati. Libro primo.* Venice: Gardane, 1546/ Rpt1554Ga, 1563Sc.

A1548Sc *Intabolatura di lautto libro secondo. Madrigali a cinque & a quattro. Canzone francese a cinque & a quattro. Motetti a cinque & a quattro. Recercari di fantasia, napolitane a quattro intabulati & accomodati per sonar di lautto per lo excellentissimo M. Julio Abondante. Novamente poste in luce & per lui medemo corretti.* Venice: Scotto, 1548.

W1548Ga *Canzon villanesche alla napolitana di messer Adriano a quatro voci con la canzon di Ruzante. Libro primo.* Venice: Gardane, 1548 (A).

W1548Sc *Canzon villanesche alla napolitana di messer Adriano a quatro voci con la canzon di Ruzante. Libro primo.* Venice: Scotto, 1548 (C,A,T,B).

P1552/7Pi   *Libro de musica de vihuela, agora nuevamente compuesto por Diego Pisador . . . Libro Septimo que trata de villanescas a tres y a quatro bozes, y dellas las tres tañidas, y la otra boz cantada por de fuera, y canciones Francesas.* Salamanca: Pisador, 1552.

W1553Ga   *Canzon villanesche alla napolitana di messer Adriano a quatro voci con la canzon di Ruzante.* Venice: Gardane, 1553 (C,A,T,B).

W1563Sc   *Madrigali a quatro voci di Adriano Willaert con alcune napolitane et la canzon de Ruzante tutte racolte insieme coretti & novamente stampati.* Venice: Scotto, 1563 (C,T,B; altus lacking).

Q1566Sc   *Il quinto libro delle villotte alla napoletana a tre voci de diversi con una todescha non piu stampato. Novamente poste in luce.* Venice: Scotto, 1566/Rpt1570Ga (C,T,B).

Other Sources Consulted

Alta.D   Antonio Altamura. *Dizionario dialettale napoletano.* Naples, 1956.

BuoniT   Tomaso Buoni. *Nuovo thesoro de' proverbi italiani.* Venice: Bernardo Giunta, 1610.

Card.C   Donna G. Cardamone. "The *Canzone villanesca alla napolitana* and Related Italian Vocal Part-Music: 1537 to 1570," 2 vols. (diss., Harvard University, 1972).

Chil.L   Oscar Chilesotti. "Note circa alcuni liutisti italiani della prima metà del Cinquecento," *Rivista musicale italiana,* 9 (1902), 36-61; 233-63.

CID   *The Cambridge Italian Dictionary.* Edited by Barbara Reynolds. Cambridge, 1962.

CW, V   *Adrian Willaert und andere Meister, italienische Madrigale zu 4-5 Stimmen. Das Chorwerk,* Vol. 5. Edited by Walter Wiora. Wolfenbüttel, n.d.

CW, VIII   *Volkstümliche italienische Lieder zu 3-4 Stimmen, A. Willaert und andere Meister. Das Chorwerk,* Vol. 8. Edited by Erich Hertzmann. Wolfenbüttel, 1930.

CW, XLIII   *Karnevalslieder der Renaissance zu 3-4 Stimmen. Das Chorwerk,* Vol. 43. Edited by Kurt Westphal. Wolfenbüttel, 1936.

Ein.IM, III   Alfred Einstein, *The Italian Madrigal,* Vol. 3. Princeton, 1949/Rpt1971.

Ein.M   Alfred Einstein. "Die mehrstimmige weltliche Musik von 1450-1600," *Handbuch der Musikgeschichte,* Vol. 1. Berlin, 1930.

EM   *Encyclopédie de la musique et dictionnaire du Conservatoire.* Edited by A. Lavignac and L. de la Laurencie. Partie I: Histoire de la musique, Vol. 2. Paris, 1931.

Flo.G   Giovanni Florio. *Giardino di ricreatione nel quale crescono fronde, fiori e frutti, vaghe, leggiadri, e soavi, sotto nome di sei mila proverbi* . . . London, Thomas Woodcock, 1591.

Hertz.W   Erich Hertzmann. *Adrian Willaert in der weltlichen Vokalmusik Italiens seiner Zeit.* Leipzig, 1931/Rpt1973.

Lov.P   Emilio Lovarini. "Una poesia musicata del Ruzzante," *Miscellanea di studi critici in onore di Vicenzo Crescini.* Cividale, 1929, pp. 237-66.

Mal.P, I   Enrico Malato. *La poesia dialettale napoletana,* Vol. 1. Naples, 1960.

NolaO, I   *Gian Domenico del Giovane da Nola: I documenti biografici e l'attività presso la SS. Annunziata con l'opera completa,* Vol. 1. Edited by Lionello Cammarota. Rome, 1973.

Rein.S, I   Ida von Reinsberg-Düringsfeld and Otto Freiherrn von Reinsberg-Düringsfeld. *Sprichwörter der germanischen und romanischen Sprachen,* Vol. 1. Leipzig, 1872.

Sper.P   Charles Speroni. "Proverbs and Proverbial Phrases in Basile's 'Pentameron'," *University of California Publications in Modern Philology,* 24 (1941), 181-288.

Zor.C   Lodovico Zorzi. "Canzoni inedite del Ruzante," *Atti dell'Istituto Veneto di Scienze, Lettere ed Arti,* 119 (1960-61), 25-74.

Critical Notes
Texts and Translations*

Songs for Four Voices

[1] *A quand'a quand'haveva una vicina* (Adriano) [Adrian Willaert] Source: S1542Sc

A quand'a quand'haveva¹ una vicina
Ch'era a² vedere la stella Diana.
Tu la vedevi
Tu li parlavi
Beato te se la basciavi tu.

Che veramente pare una regina
Ogn'uno³ ne faria inamorare.⁴
Tu la vedevi
Tu li parlavi
Beato te se la basciavi tu.

Che quando se levava la matina
Phebo per scorno se ne ritornava.
Tu la vedevi
Tu li parlavi
Beato te se la basciavi tu.

Mo mi credeva starne⁵ contento
Et trovomi le mani pien di vento.
Tu la vedevi
Tu li parlavi
Beato te se la basciavi tu.

(Oh once I had a neighbor
Who looked like the morning star Diana.
You've seen her,
You've spoken to her,
You're lucky if you've kissed her.

Truly she looked like a queen
And could make anybody love her.
You've seen her,
You've spoken to her,
You're lucky if you've kissed her.

For in the morning when she arose
The moon, disgraced, withdrew once more.
You've seen her,
You've spoken to her,
You're lucky if you've kissed her.

Just when I thought I was in paradise,
I found myself empty-handed.
You've seen her,
You've spoken to her,
You're lucky if you've kissed her.)

TEXT: S1542Sc: 4 strophes; W1545Ga, W1548Ga, W1548Sc, W1553Ga—strophes 1, 2, 4; W1544Sc,

W1563Sc—strophe 1; S1542Sc—the music is underlaid with the texts of all four strophes.
 1. W1545Ga, W1548Ga, W1548Sc, W1553Ga: havea.
 2. W1545Ga, W1548Ga, W1548Sc, W1553Ga, W1563Sc: Ch'er'a.
 3. W1545Ga, W1548Ga, W1548Sc: Ch'ogni uno.
 4. W1548Ga, W1548Sc, W1553Ga: innamorare.
 5. W1545Ga, W1548Ga, W1548Sc, W1553Ga: stare.
This line has only ten syllables, probably because the word de was omitted after credeva.

MUSIC: Cantus has the rubric, "In diapason, si placet" in S1542Sc, W1563Sc; altus located in the tenor partbook in S1542Sc, W1563Sc, corrected in W1545Ga, W1548Ga, W1548Sc, W1553Ga; tenor located in the altus partbook in S1542Sc, [W1563Sc]. M. 18, bassus, note 6 is C in S1542Sc, W1545Ga, W1548Sc, W1553Ga, W1563Sc.

[2] *Buccucia dolce chiù che canamielle* (Piersson) [Perissone Cambio] Source: W1548Sc

Buccucia dolce chiù che canamielle¹
Labruccia d'una pampana di rosa.
Hai scropolosa
S'io cerco un baso
Rispondi: ba ca marzo te l'a raso.²

Lassa signora homai d'esser crudele³
Non ti mostrar ver me tanto sdegnosa.
Hai scropolosa
S'io cerco un baso
Rispondi: ba ca marzo te l'a raso.

Baciame una sol volta e sta sicura
Bocha basciata mai perde ventura.⁴
Hai scropolosa
S'io cerco un baso
Rispondi: ba ca marzo te l'a raso.

(Oh little mouth sweeter than sugar cane,
Softer than the petals of a rose.
You're so scrupulous,
If I try for a kiss
You say: "Watch out or March will get you."

Leave off being cruel to me, lady,
Stop behaving in that haughty fashion.
You're so scrupulous,
If I try for a kiss
You say: "Watch out or March will get you."

Kiss me just once for I promise that
A kissed mouth never loses its luck.
You're so scrupulous,
If I try for a kiss
You say: "Watch out or March will get you.")

*The poems were translated by Theodolinda Barolini and Donna G. Cardamone.

TEXT: W1548Sc, W1548Ga, W1553Ga—3 strophes.

1. This line is related to an Italian proverb, "E più dolce che'l miele" (Sper.P, 234); chiù is Neapolitan for più.

2. In the *Pentamerone* (Second Diversion of the Fifth Day, "The Months"), Giambattista Basile cites this line as an example of a proverb used to break unfortunate news: "March has ruined you" or literally, "March has shaved you." March is portrayed in this tale, on the one hand, as a cursed month of unpleasant weather which stirs up ill humors. For other sources of the proverb see Sper.P, 240. According to Giambattista Del Tufo, a Neapolitan cavalier, this proverb was widely quoted in sixteenth-century Naples. In a chapter of his *Ritratto . . . della nobilissima città di Napoli* (1588) entitled "Parlar goffo della plebe napolitana," he quotes a typical response to a liar: "Va figlio mio, ca Marzo te ne rase de vennerme cetrule pe cerase," or "Go away my boy or March will get you for selling me cucumbers for cherries." See also the closing couplet of "Tu pur ti pensi," a *strambotto* in Neapolitan dialect in *Madrigali a tre et arie napolitane* [Rome: Dorico, ca. 1550], no. 19.

3. W1553Ga: crudelle.

4. This line is part of an Italian proverb, "Bocca basciata non perde ventura, anzi si rinuova come fa la luna" (Flo.D, 18).

MUSIC: M. 5, altus, note 3 is e'-flat in W1548Sc, W1548Ga, W1553Ga. M. 14, altus, note 1 is e'-flat in W1548Sc, W1548Ga, W1553Ga. M. 20, altus, note 3 has a sharp before e' in W1548Sc, W1548Ga, W1553Ga. M. 28, altus, note 4 is b in W1553Ga.

[3] *Cingari simo venit'a giocare* (Adriano) [Adrian Willaert] Source: W1545Ga

Cingari simo venit'a[1] giocare
Donn'alla[2] coriolla de bon core.
   Ch'el è dentro ch'el è fuore[3]
   S'el è dentr'ha più sapore.

Calate iuso per ve solazare
Ca iocarimo un po per vostr'amore.
   Ch'el è dentro ch'el è fuore
   S'el è dentr'ha più sapore.

Se noi perdiamo pagamo un carlino
E se perdete voi pagate il vino.
   Ch'el è dentro ch'el è fuore
   S'el è dentr'ha più sapore.

(We are gypsies come to play
The game called Queen of Hearts.
   This one's in — that one's out,
   It's more fun when round about.

Come on down and have some fun
As we gamble a little for your love.
   This one's in — that one's out,
   It's more fun when round about.

If we lose, we'll pay a carlino,[4]
And if you lose, you'll buy the wine.
   This one's in — that one's out,
   It's more fun when round about.)

TEXT: W1545Ga, W1548Sc, W1548Ga, W1553Ga—3 strophes; W1544Sc, W1563Sc—only strophe 1.

1. W1548Sc, W1548Ga, W1553Ga: venite'a.

2. W1548Sc, W1548Ga, W1553Ga: donne'alle.

3. W1548Sc: fuora.

4. carlino: name given to silver coins of various values formerly current in Naples (Alta.D, 97).

MUSIC: Key signature has two B-flats in cantus in W1563Sc. M. 11, bassus, note 4 has no flat in W1563Sc. M. 19 and m. 25, bassus, note 7 has no flat in W1563Sc. M. 20, tenor, note 2 is c' in W1563Sc. M. 20 and m. 26, bassus, note 3 is f, note 4 is e in W1563Sc. M. 22 and m. 28, bassus, note 7 has no flat in W1563Sc. Mod. ed. in Ein.M, 370.

[4] *Le vecchie per invidia sono pazze* (Fran. Corteccia) [Francesco Corteccia] Source: W1545Ga

Le vecchie per invidia sono pazze
Dicendo quella bella mal nasciuta.
   Come son pazze
   Ste vecchie canazze.

(The old crones are wild with envy,
For them a beauty is always a whore.
   How crazy they are,
   These old bitches.)

TEXT: W1545Ga, W1548Ga, W1548Sc, W1553Ga—one strophe.
No variants.

MUSIC: No. [4] is attributed to Willaert in W1548Sc, W1548Ga, W1553Ga; for evidence to support Corteccia's authorship, see Hertz.W, 76. M. 1, cantus, mensuration sign is C in W1545Ga, W1548Sc, W1553Ga.

[5] *Madonna mia famme bon'offerta* (Adriano) [Adrian Willaert] Source: W1545Ga

Madonna mia famme bon'offerta
Ch'io porto per presente[1] sto galuccio.[2]
   Che sempre canta quand'è dì alle galline[3]
   E dice: chi chir chi
   E tanto calca forte la galina[4]
   Che li fa nascer l'ov'ogni matina.[5]

Quisto[6] mio galo[7] sempre sta al'alerta
Quando il dì dorme sotto la coperta.
   Che sempre canta quand'è dì alle galline
   E dice: chi chir chi
   E tanto calca forte la galina
   Che li fa nascer l'ov'ogni matina.

Presto madonna se lo voi vedere
Ca te lo facio[8] mo quisto[9] piacere.
   Che sempre canta quand'è dì alle galline
   E dice: chi chir chi
   E tanto calca forte la galina
   Che li fa nascer l'ov'ogni matina.

(My lady, make me a good offer
And in return I'll bring you this fat cock.
He crows to tell the hens it's day,
"Chi chir, chi," he'll always say.
So hard does he tread the hen,
She lays an egg each day at ten.

This cock of mine is always watchful,
Even in the daytime asleep under cover.
He crows to tell the hens it's day,
"Chi chir chi," he'll always say.
So hard does he tread the hen,
She lays an egg each day at ten.

Be quick, my lady, if you want to see him
Because I offer you this treat right now.
He crows to tell the hens it's day,
"Chi chir chi," he'll always say.
So hard does he tread the hen,
She lays an egg each day at ten.)

TEXT: W1545Ga, W1548Ga, W1548Sc, W1553Ga—3 strophes; W1544Sc, W1563Sc—strophe 1.
1. The word "presente" in the sense of "dono" or gift is also found in the comedies of Angelo Beolco (Ruzante), a Paduan (Zor.C, 64).
2. The strutting, vainglorious cock is a common figure in Italian folklore. His song represents the command to love which the hen must obligingly obey. She, on the other hand, has no equivalent song — only a chirp to call her brood of chicks (BuoniT, 33). The following proverb, which warns married women to maintain an obedient silence, is an example of the popular personification of the hen and cock: "Trista è quella casa, ove la gallina canta, e il gallo tace" or "Sad is that home where the hen sings and the cock is silent" (Flo.G, 201).
3. W1548Sc: galine.
4. W1548Ga, W1553Ga, W1563Sc: gallina.
5. W1553Ga, W1563Sc: mattina.
6. W1548Sc, W1548Ga, W1553Ga: quisso.
7. W1548Sc, W1548Ga, W1553Ga: gallo.
8. W1553Ga: faccio.
9. W1548Sc, W1548Ga, W1553Ga: quisso.

MUSIC: M. 1, cantus, key signature has two B-flats in W1563Sc. M. 2, tenor, note 3 is b-flat in W1545Ga, W1548Sc, W1553Ga, W1563Sc. M. 3, cantus, beats 1 and 2 rhythm, minim, 2 semiminims in W1563Sc. M. 6, bassus, note 4 is B-flat in W1545Ga, W1563Sc. M. 7, bassus, note 1 is c in W1545Ga, W1563Sc. M. 24 and m. 27, cantus, note 4 is a minim in W1563Sc. M. 25 and m. 28, cantus, note 1 is a semiminim in W1563Sc.

[6] *Madonna mia io son un poverello* (Anon.) Source: W1545Ga; unicum

Madonna mia io son un poverello
Cerco patron et chiamomi Martino.[1]
Come son fino
Provam'un poco per ogni loco
Come ti servo da ser'et mattino
Et chiamomi Martino.

(My lady, I'm just a poor guy
Seeking a mistress and my name is Martino.
Give me a try,
You'll see in every way how sharp I am;
I'll serve you night and day,
And my name is Martino.)

TEXT: 1. In Neapolitan dialect Martino, besides being a proper name, is slang for *cornuto* (cuckold) or *coltello* (knife); see Mal.P, I, 657.

MUSIC: Another setting of the same poem may be found in *Di Antonio Barges il primo libro de villotte a quatro voci* (Venice: A. Gardane, 1550), p. 6. The only relationship between the settings is Barges' brief quotation of the opening phrase of the tune in the tenor. M. 10, altus, note 5 is d' in W1545Ga.

[7] *Madonn'io non lo so perchè lo fai* (Adriano) [Adrian Willaert] Source: W1545Ga

Madonn'io non lo so perchè lo fai
Che me ti mostr'in tutto scorrucciata.[1]
Perchè sei cos'ingrata[2]
Se sai per te son cieco
Dolor sta sempre meco.

O Dio famme n'escir de tanti guai
Ca non g'incamparaggio[3] un'altra fiata.
Perchè sei cos'ingrata
Se sai per te son cieco
Dolor sta sempre meco.

O mora o camp'hormai non me ne curo
Sto mondo latr'è fatto a chi ha ventura.
Perchè sei cos'ingrata
Se sai per te son cieco
Dolor sta sempre meco.

(My lady, I don't know why you do it,
Why are you always so angry about everything?
Why are you so ungrateful?
You know because of you I'm blind
And always filled with heartache.

Oh God, let me out of such troubles,
Because I won't live with them another moment.
Why are you so ungrateful?
You know because of you I'm blind
And always filled with heartache.

I don't give a damn by now if I live or die;
One needs luck to make it in this world of thieves.
Why are you so ungrateful?
You know because of you I'm blind
And always filled with heartache.)

TEXT: W1545Ga, W1548Ga, W1548Sc, W1553Ga—3 strophes; W1544Sc, W1563Sc—strophe 1
1. W1563Sc: scorucciata.
2. W1553Ga: cosi ingrata.
3. Neapolitan verb form: first person future, first conjugation (Alta.D, 22).

Music: M. 1, cantus, key signature has two B-flats in W1563Sc. M. 4, cantus, note 4 is f' in W1563Sc. Mod. ed. in CW, VIII, 18.

[8] *Madonn'io t'haggi amat'et amo assai* (Fran. Corteccia) [Francesco Corteccia] Source: W1545Ga (unicum)

Madonn'io t'haggi[1] amat'et amo assai
Et mai non mi volesti consolare.
Et sempre d'ogg'in crai[2]
Cra cra cra fa la cornachia
Et alle pene mia fine non sacchia.

(My lady, I loved you and still love you very much,
Yet you have never wanted to comfort me.
As the day is long 'til tomorrow,
Caw caw caw croaks the crow
Mindless of my aching woe.)

Text: 1. Neapolitan verb form, haggio: avere, first person present (Alta.D, 21).
2. Crai can also be used to represent the voice of the crow (CID, 204). According to the word play, the crow here personifies a chatterbox whose tedious procrastinations frustrate her lover. The crow is frequently personified in Italian proverbs and popular sayings (BuoniT, 315).

Music: Another setting of the same poem may be found in *Di Antonio Barges il primo libro de villotte*, p. 5. It is likely that Corteccia and Barges based their compositions upon the same song model, now lost, because the tune is the same in both settings. However, in Barges' setting it migrates between the cantus and tenor, and in Corteccia's it remains in the cantus. M. 2, all parts, note 2 is a semibreve in W1545Ga. M. 3, tenor, final note is c' in W1545Ga. M. 4, all parts, a double bar separates the couplet from the refrain in W1545Ga. M. 15, cantus, notes 1 and 2 omitted in W1545Ga.

[9] *O bene mio fam'uno favore* (Adriano) [Adrian Willaert] Source: S1542Sc

O bene mio fam'uno[1] favore
Che questa sera ti possa parlare.
E s'alcuno ti ci trova
E tu grida: chi vend'ova.

Vieni[2] senza paura e non bussare
Butta la porta che porai entrare.
E s'alcuno ti ci trova
E tu grida: chi vend'ova.

Alla finestra insino alle due hore
Farò la spia che porai entrare.
E s'alcuno ti ci trova
E tu grida: chi vend'ova.

(Oh love of mine do me just one favor
So that we can be together tonight.
And if anyone should see you while you're here,
Just yell out, "Who's selling eggs?"

Come without fear and don't knock,
Push the door open and walk right in,
And if anyone should see you while you're here,
Just yell out, "Who's selling eggs?"

I'll spy at the window until two-o-clock
Just to make sure you can come in,
And if anyone should see you while you're here,
Just yell out, "Who's selling eggs?")

Text: S1542Sc, W1545Ga, W1548Ga, W1548Sc, W1553Ga—3 strophes; W1563Sc—strophe 1. S1542Sc: the music is underlaid with the texts of all three strophes.
   1. W1545Ga, W1548Ga, W1548Sc, W1553Ga, W1563Sc: famm'uno.
   2. W1545Ga, W1548Ga, W1548Sc, W1553Ga: viene.

Music: Cantus has the rubric "In diapason, si placet" in S1542Sc, W1563Sc; cantus, mensuration sign is C in W1548Sc; altus, clef is on the third line in W1545Ga, W1548Ga, W1548Sc, W1553Ga. M. 17, tenor, note 1 is c' in W1553Ga. Mod. ed. in CW, V, 61 (transposed up a fourth).

[10] *O Dio si vede chiaro cha per te moro* (Fran. Silvestrino) [Francesco Silvestrino] Source: W1545Ga

O Dio si vede chiaro cha per te moro
Perchè me stracii haime sì fieramente.
Mirate o gente
Come mi trata[1] mal questa crudele.

Meschino a me sai ben quanto ti adoro
Et penar mi vuoi far sì stranamente.
Mirate o gente
Come mi trata mal questa crudele.

Dhe per pietà vita della mia vita
Dona a me che ti adoro qualche aita.
Mirate o gente
Come me trata mal questa crudele.

(Oh God! It's so obvious that I'm dying for you,
Why must you tear at me so fiercely?
Look everyone,
See how badly this cruel woman treats me.

I'm so miserable! You know well how much I adore you,
And yet you make me suffer so outlandishly.
Look everyone,
See how badly this cruel woman treats me.

For pity's sake! Life of my life,
Give some help to the one who so adores you.
Look everyone,
See how badly this cruel woman treats me.)

Text: W1545Ga, W1548Ga, W1548Sc, W1553Ga—3 strophes.
   1. W1548Sc, W1548Ga, W1553Ga: tratta.

Music: M. 10, all parts, mensuration sign is 3 with coloration in W1545Ga, W1548Ga, W1548Sc, W1553Ga. M. 11, cantus, tenor, and bassus, mensuration sign is C and no sign in altus in W1553Ga.

[11] *O dolce vita mia che t'haggio fatto* (Adriano) [Adrian Willaert] Source: W1545Ga

O dolce vita mia che t'haggio fatto
Che mi minacci ogn'hor con tue parolle.
 Et io mi struggo come nev'al sole.

Se sai ca per tuo amor son quasi morto
C'a te del arder mio niente ti dole.[1]
 Et io mi struggo come nev'al sole.

Mo son perduto e tengomi disfatto
Che m'hai mandato a coglier[2] le viole.
 Et io mi struggo come nev'al sole.

(Sweet light of my life, what have I done
That makes you constantly threaten me?
 Like snow in the sun I am ever more consumed.

You must know that I'm almost dead for love of you,
Since my burning desire causes you no pain.
 Like snow in the sun I am ever more consumed.

Now I'm lost and I know I'm undone
Because you've sent me out to pick posies.
 Like snow in the sun I am ever more consumed.)

Text: W1545Ga, W1548Ga, W1548Sc, W1553Ga—3 strophes.
 1. W1548Sc: duole.
 2. W1548Sc: coglier'.

Music: M. 10, cantus, note 4 is a' in W1548Sc, W1553Ga. Mod. eds. in CW, VIII, 16; Ein.IM, III, 88.

[12] *Occhio non fu giamai che lachrimasse* (Adriano) [Adrian Willaert] Source: W1563Sc (facsimile in Zor.C, Plates VI, VII); unicum

Occhio non fu giamai che lachrimasse
Con sì rason de doia da morire.
 O car'amore,
 O bell'amore,
 O dolc'amore,
 O fin'amore,
 Che tien il mondo inamorà,
 Hai corona di quanti amor fu ma'.

(Never has there been an eye that could weep
With such good reason from the pain of dying.
 Oh dear love,
 Oh beautiful love,
 Oh tender love,
 Oh pure love,
 Who held the world enamoured.
 Ah! Crowning glory of any love that has ever lived.)

Text: This composition is listed in the *tavola* under the rubic "Canzon di Ruzante," together with "Quando di rose d'oro" (no. [13]) and "Zoia zentil" (no. [20]). Longer versions of all three poems with more extensive use of Paduan dialect can be found in Venice, Biblioteca Marciana, ms. ital. classe IX, n. 271 (collocazione 6096). They have been attributed to Ruzante on the basis of internal stylistic evidence (Zor.C, 62-70). "Occhio non fu" has six strophes which was probably its original form (Zor.C, 39-40). Each strophe contains a recurrent refrain with a changing penultimate line, e.g., strophes 1 and 2:

Occhio non fu zà mai che lagremasse
Co' sì rason de dogia da morire,
Quanto gi uogi dolenti del mio cuore,
Daspò che morte m'ha robà el me amore.
 O caro amore,
 O dolce amore,
 O bello amore,
 O fin'amore,
 Che tegnia el mondo inamorà,
 Ahi, ahi, corona de quanti amor fu ma'.

Amor mio, ti eri el fior del Paradiso;
Nascesti per ventura in fra la zente,
Tutta vestita de celestiale,
Tu gieri un'anzoletta con le ale.
 O caro amore,
 O dolce amore,
 O bell'amore,
 O fin'amore,
 Che via sì presto tu te si volà,
 Ahi, ahi, corona de quanti amor fu ma'.

A variant of the first strophe was set to music by Filippo Azzaiuolo, *Il primo libro de villotte alla padoana . . .* (Venice: A. Gardane, 1557), p. 19 (facsimile in Zor.C, Plates VIII, IX):

Occhio non fu giamai che lagrimasse
Così ragion di doglia di morire.
Fa la li le la.
O quanto gl'occhi dolenti del mio core,
Da po' che morte m'ha robbà il mio amore.
 O car'amore,
 O dolc'amore,
 O bell'amore,
 O fin'amore,
 Che tien il mondo innamorà,
 Tu sei collonna di quant'amor fu mai.

Still another variant of this poem can be found in a printed miscellany of popular poetry (Venice, Biblioteca Marciana, misc. 2213.6): *Due canzon nove bellissime da cantare . . .* [Venice: Domenico de Franceschi, 1585], fol. 1v. The text was probably extracted from a musical setting because certain words and verse lines are repeated, e.g., strophe 1:

Ochii non fui, non fui giamai che lachrimasse
Come ragion de doglia di morire, di morire.
 O bel'amore,
 O car'amore,
 O dolc'amore,
 O fin'amore,
 Che tien el mondo, el mondo innamorà.
 Che tien el mondo, el mondo innamorà.

This version, like the one set by Willaert, lacks lines 3 and 4 of the opening quatrain. It is effectively a *villanesca* with an opening unrhymed couplet of 11-syllable lines and a recurrent unchanging refrain. The lines that were omitted reveal that the poem was originally a lament on the death of a loved one: "Or a heart that could bleed as much as mine, since death has stolen my beloved from me."

MUSIC: The altus partbook is missing; altus composed by the editor. M. 16, tenor, repeat sign omitted in W1563Sc. M. 36, cantus, note 1 is a breve in W1563Sc.

[13] *Quando di rose d'oro* (Adriano) [Adrian Willaert]
    Source: W1563Sc; unicum

Quando di rose d'oro
Vien l'alb'incoronata,
Con trezze di thresoro
Bagnà d'acqua rosata.
Et co'l so bel venire
Porta 'l dolce dromire.

(When the blush of dawn approaches,
It is crowned with gilt-edged roses,
Adorned with shining tresses
Newly bathed in rosy dew.
With the rich unfolding morn
Comes a sweetly-scented slumber.)

TEXT: Attributed to Ruzante (see no. [12]). For Ruzante's poem of 14 strophes in the form of an amorous dialogue, see Zor. C, 37-9.

MUSIC: The altus partbook is missing; altus composed by the editor.

[14] *Se mille volte ti vengh'a vedere* (Fran. Silvestrino) [Francesco Silvestrino] Source: W1545Ga; unicum

Se mille volte ti vengh'a vedere
Tu mille volte mostri star sdegnosa.
    O bella rosa o giglio matutino
    Vedi'l meschino ca per te si more.

Et s'io non vengo ti dimostri havere
Gravi tormenti et stai sempre dogliosa.
    O bella rosa o giglio matutino
    Vedi'l meschino ca per te si more.

Se mi ami o se non m'ami dimel chiaro
Che questa volta alla mie spese imparo.
    O bella rosa o giglio matutino
    Vedi'l meschino ca per te si more.

(A thousand times I come to see you
And a thousand times you scorn me.
    Oh beautiful rose, oh morning lily,
    Look at the poor fellow who dies for you.

But if I don't come, you seem tormented
By constant grief and pain.
    Oh beautiful rose, oh morning lily,
    Look at the poor fellow who dies for you.

Whether you love me or not, tell me outright
For no matter what it costs, this time I want to know.
    Oh beautiful rose, oh morning lily,
    Look at the poor fellow who dies for you.)

TEXT: No errors.

MUSIC: M. 16, bassus, note 7 is c in W1545Ga. M. 28, all parts, mensuration sign is 3 in W1545Ga. M. 34, altus, note 1 is f'-sharp in W1545Ga.

[15] *Sempre mi ride sta donna da bene* (Adriano) [Adrian Willaert] Source: W1545Ga

Sempre mi ride sta donna da bene
Quando passeggio per mezo sta via.
    La riderella
    La pazzarella
    Non vi ca ride
    Ha ha ha ridemo tutti per darli piacere.

(This courtesan always laughs at me
When I walk down this street.
    The silly flirt,
    The crazy lady
    Can only laugh;
    Ha, ha, ha, let's all laugh to make her happy.)

TEXT: W1545Ga, W1548Ga, W1548Sc, W1553Ga—one strophe. No variants.

MUSIC: M. 7, altus, note 4 is f' in W1548Sc. M. 9, altus, the sharp is placed after note 5 in W1545Ga. M. 38, beat 3 and M. 39, beat 1, rhythm: semiminim, dotted semiminim, semifusa, semifusa, semiminim in W1553Ga.

[16] *Si come bella sei fosti pietosa* (Fran. Silvestrino) [Francesco Silvestrino] Source: W1545Ga; unicum

Si come bella sei fosti pietosa
Al mondo non saria 'na simul cosa.
    Anima mia
    Ch'io per te mille volte moreria
    Gioiela mia.

Beata te cor mio tu sei la bella
Fra tutte l'altre te ne puoi vantare.
    Anima mia
    Ch'io per te mille volte moreria
    Gioiela mia.

Ma più bellezza in te donna saria
Se contentaste alla gran pena mia.
    Anima mia
    Ch'io per te mille volte moreria
    Gioiela mia.

(If you were as merciful as you are beautiful
You could not be surpassed the whole world over.
    Soul of mine,
    I'd die for you a thousand times,
    My treasure.

Your beauty is such, my love,
That midst all other women you can vaunt it.
Soul of mine,
I'd die for you a thousand times,
My treasure.

But there would be even more beauty in you, lady,
If you would ease my extreme pain.
Soul of mine,
I'd die for you a thousand times,
My treasure.)

Text: No errors.

Music: M. 12, altus, note 1 is a dotted minim in W1545Ga.

[17] *Sospiri miei d'oime doglioririosi et senz'aita* (Adriano) [Adrian Willaert] Source: W1545Ga

Sospiri miei d'oime doglioririosi et senz'aita
Deh partitevi da me cangiate loco.
Do che ti giova (do ri don) esser sì bella
Son¹ (fa ru ra ru rella)² vuoi ben'a me.
Sappi chi non ha bene in gioventù d'in amar oime
Stent'in vecchiezza (to ri ron) amaritudine.³
Son (fa ru ra ru rella) vuoi ben'a me.

(Sorrowful sighs, alas, which cannot be subdued
Pray, leave me and find another dwelling.
What good does it do you (do ri don) to be so beautiful
If you don't (fa ru ra ru rella) love me?
Remember that he who doesn't love well in youth, alas,
Spends his old age (to ri ron) in bitterness.
So it will be for you (fa ru ra ru rella) if you don't love me.)

Text: W1545Ga, W1548Ga, W1548Sc, W1553Ga—one strophe.
1. Son: se non.
2. W1548Ga, W1548Sc, W1553Ga: riella (see also line 7).
3. Related to an Italian proberb, "Chi non fa ben in gioventù, stenta in vecchiezza" (Rein.S, I, no. 847).

Music: Mm. 26 and 34, cantus, note 1 is f'-sharp in W1553Ga. M. 36, tenor, note 1, dot omitted in W1548Sc.

[18] *Un giorno mi pregò una vedovella* (Adriano) [Adrian Willaert] Source: W1545Ga

Un giorno mi pregò una vedovella
D'andar un dur scoglio con lei passare.
Navigando su la sua navicella
Con arte il timon sa ben governare.
Ma con la lingua intriga
Gridando barca sia
Sta lì tien duro voga
Prem'a¹ sta bona via.

Co'l rem'in mezo mi miss'a vogare
A lei molto piacque 'l mio gran stentare.
Co'l vent'in poppa pensai d'anegare

Ma m'aiutò da Berghem mio compare.
Et sospirando dissi
Deh cara vedovella
Così tratti gl'amici
Su la tua navicella.

(One day a sweet widow beseeched me
To help her sail by a dangerous reef.
"A rudder is needed," she argued,
"To skillfully guide my little boat."
But then with her deceptive tongue
She yelled: "Keep rowing harder,
Don't stop!
Press on in this direction."
With the oar in the middle I began to row
And my immense exertion pleased her greatly.
With the wind blowing to the rear I was sure I'd drown,
But a friend from Bergamo came to my aid.
When it was over I said with a sigh,
"Pray tell, dear widow,
Is this how you treat friends
On your little boat?")

Text: W1544Sc, W1545Ga, W1548Ga, W1548Sc, W1553Ga: one strophe.
1. W1548Ga, W1548Sc, W1553Ga: premi'a.

Music: M. 1, tenor, mensuration sign is C3 in W1553Ga. M. 7, tenor, beat 1, no coloration in W1548Sc. M. 9, cantus, note 2 is breve (b'-flat) in W1545Ga, W1548Sc, W1553Ga. M. 20, all parts, mensuration sign is ₵ in W1544Sc, W1545Ga, W1548Ga, W1548Sc, W1553Ga. M. 33, all parts, mensuration sign is ₵3 in W1545Ga, W1548Ga, W1548Sc, W1553Ga. Similarly, mensuration sign is $\phi\frac{3}{2}$ in W1544Sc. M. 42, altus, beat 2 is breve-rest in W1545Ga. M. 46, tenor, no coloration in W1548Sc. Mm. 60-1, tenor, no coloration on g, a in W1548Sc; ligature included only g, a in W1553Ga. M. 62, all parts, mensuration sign is ₵3 in W1545Ga, W1548Ga, W1548Sc, W1553Ga; mensuration sign is $\phi\frac{3}{2}$ in W1544Sc. Mm. 64-5, altus and tenor, binaria ligature with "Deh, deh" in W1553Ga. M. 74, all parts, mensuration sign is ₵3 in W1545Ga, W1548Ga, W1548Sc, W1553Ga; mensuration sign is ϕ 3/2 in W1544Sc. M. 77, tenor, no coloration in W1548Sc. Mod. ed. in CW, VIII, 5.

[19] *Vecchie letrose non valete niente* (Adriano) [Adrian Willaert] Source: W1545Ga

Vecchie letrose¹ non valete niente
Se non a far l'aguaito per la chiazza.
Tira alla mazza
Vecchie letrose scannaros'e² pazze.

(Sullen old hags are good for nothing
But setting traps for lovers in the public square.
Go ahead and club them,
Those scabrous, crazy old cut-throats.)

Text: W1544Sc, W1545Ga, W1548Ga, W1548Sc, W1553Ga—one strophe.

1. W1544Sc: retrose.

2. W1553Ga: scannarose e.

MUSIC: No variants.

[20] *Zoia zentil che per secreta via* (Adriano) [Adrian Willaert] Source: W1548Sc

Zoia zentil che per secreta via
Ten vai di cuor in cuore[1]
Portando la legrezza[2] de l'amore.
Col[3] to venir celato
Tanto ben m'hai portato
Che per legrezza tanta
El m'è forza che canta:
Fa li le li lon.

Beato colui son
Ch'a lo so amor in don.
L'amor n'è ben n'è caro
Che s'ha col so danaro.
Pì ch'el[4] se paga manco[5] è da stimare:
L'amor donato non si po[6] pagare.

(Gentle joy, you go by secret ways
From heart to heart
Carrying the joy of love.
You've brought me such happiness
With your secret coming
And such joy that
I am compelled to sing:
Fa li le li lon.

Fortunate is the one
Who receives love as a gift.
Love obtained with money
Is neither decent nor precious.
The more you pay, the less it's worth:
Love freely given cannot be bought.)

TEXT: W1548Sc, W1548Ga, W1553Ga, W1563Sc—one strophe; facsimile of W1563Sc in Zor.C, Plates V, VII.

1. W1548Ga, W1553Ga, W1563Sc: di cor in core.

2. W1548Ga, W1563Sc: legrezze; W1553Ga: l'allegrezze.

3. W1563Sc: co'l.

4. W1563Sc: che'l.

5. W1553Ga: mancho; W1563Sc: manch'e.

6. W1563Sc: puo.

"Zoia zentil" is attributed to Ruzante in each partbook of W1548Sc and W1553Ga (except bassus). The attribution is not given with the music in W1563Sc; rather the piece is listed with "Occhio non fu" and "Quando di rose d'oro" in the *tavola* under the heading "Canzon di Ruzante." Confirmation of Ruzante's authorship is given in Zor.C, 62-70, and Lov.P, 250-66. The complete poem of three strophes is given below from the only other known source: Venice, Biblioteca Marciana, ms. ital. classe IX, n. 271 (collocazione 6096), fols. 87-87v. This version, probably the original, contains more words in Paduan dialect and may well have been sung to Willaert's music during his lifetime. The second and third strophes can be underlaid with little difficulty to the score printed in this edition.

1. Zuogia zentil che per secretta via
   Ten vai de cuor in cuor'
   Portando le legrezze
   Le legrezze dell'amore.
   Co'l tuo vegnir celato
   Tanto ben m'hai portato
   Che per legrezza tanta
   El m'è forza che canta:
   Tan dan da ri ron de la.

   Beato colui son
   Ch'ha lo so amor in don.
   L'amor n'è bel n'è caro
   Co'l s'ha col so dinaro.
   Pì che'l se paga manco è da stimare:
   L'amor donato non se puol pagare.

2. Quanto thesoro quanta richezza mai
   'Brazza l'onde del mare
   Non mi faria zà mai
   El to nome apalentar.
   Basta che l'è la fiore
   D'ogni lezadro amore
   Pensa chi sa pensare
   S'ho rason de cantare:
   Tan dan da ri ron de la.

   Chi vuol l'amor zoioso
   Sappia tegnirlo ascoso.
   Ma chi lo vuol dolente
   Fazza accorta la zente.
   L'amor palese non è da stimare:
   L'amor secretto non se puol pagare.

3. La più bella corona ch'abbia el sole
   Si son le chiare stelle
   Gi uogi de lo mio amore
   Si son di quelle.
   El so viso zentile
   Par un mazo d'avrile.
   Né d'altro no me vanto
   Ma torno su 'l me canto:
   Tan dan da ri ron de la.

   El so fresco colore
   Non vien da depentore
   Ma dalle matutine
   Ruosette senza spine.
   Ché'l contrafatto amor n'è da stimare:
   L'amor chi è schietto non si puol pagare.

1. (Gentle joy, you go by secret ways
   From heart to heart
   Carrying the joys of love.
   You've brought me such happiness
   With your secret coming
   And such joy that
   I am compelled to sing:
   Tan dan da ri ron de la.

Fortunate is the one
Who receives love as a gift.
Love obtained with money
Is neither decent nor precious.
The more you pay, the less it's worth.
Love freely given cannot be bought.

2. All the treasures, all the riches
Embraced by the waves of the sea
Could never make me
Reveal your name.
It is enough that you are the flower
Of every gracious love.
Let one who can reason
Wonder if I have the right to sing:
Tan dan da ri ron de la.

He who wants joyful love
Must know how to keep it hidden.
But he who wants it painful
Need only let the world know.
Love revealed is worth nothing:
Secret love cannot be bought.

3. The sun's most beautiful crown,
Like the bright stars
Are the very things
Of which my beloved's eyes are made.
Her gentle face is like
A bouquet of April's flowers.
I'll boast of nothing else
But turn instead to my song:
Tan dan da ri ron de la.

The fresh color of her face
Comes not from paint
But from the thornless
Roses of the dawn.
Artificial love is worth nothing:
True love cannot be bought.)

MUSIC: Mm. 13-14 and 17-18, bassus, ligature omitted in W1563Sc. Mm. 14 and 18, tenor, ligature present in W1563Sc. M. 26, bassus, note 4 is f in W1563Sc. M. 27, altus and bassus, ligature present in W1563Sc. M. 31, bassus, note 1 is semiminim in W1548Sc. Mod. ed. in CW, VIII, 8.

Three-Voice Song Models

[21] *Cingari simo venit'a giocare* (Nola) [Gian Domenico da Nola] Source: N1545/1Ga

Cingari simo venit'a giocare
Donn'alla coriola de bon core,
    Ch'ell'è dentro ch'ell'è fore
    Quand'è dentro ha più sapore.

Calate iuso[1] per ve solazare
Ca iocarimo un po per vostr'amore.
    Ch'ell'è dentro ch'ell'è fore
    Quand'è dentro ha più sapore.

Et ve mettimo per ve contentare
Quisto bastone[2] in mano a tutte l'ore.
    Ch'ell'è dentro ch'ell'è fore
    Quand'è dentro ha più sapore.

Se noi perdimo pagamo un carlino[3]
E se perdite voi pagate il vino.
    Ch'ell'è dentro ch'ell'è fore
    Quand'è dentro ha più sapore.

(We are gypsies come to play
The game called Queen of Hearts.
    This one's in — that one's out,
    It's more fun when round about.

Come on down and have some fun
As we gamble a little for your love.
    This one's in — that one's out,
    It's more fun when round about.

To keep you happy, we'll make sure
You have this club in your hands all the time.
    This one's in — that one's out,
    It's more fun when round about.

If we lose, we'll pay a carlino,
And if you lose, you'll buy the wine.
    This one's in — that one's out,
    It's more fun when round about.)

TEXT:
1. iuso: Neapolitan for giù (Alta.D, 132).
2. In the Venetian card pack, bastoni are clubs (CID, 86).
3. See no. [3], n. 4.

MUSIC: No printing errors. Mod. eds. in CW, XLIII, 13; NolaO, I, 97.

[22] *Madonn'io non lo so perchè lo fai* (Nola) [Gian Domenico da Nola] Source: N1545/1Ga

Madonn'io non lo so perchè lo fai
Che me ti mostr'in tutto scorrocciata.
    Perchè sei cos'ingrata
    Se sai per te son cieco
    Dolor sta sempre meco.

Non so che nelle[1] ciocchie[2] posto t'ai
Farme morire so che ben t'è grata.
    Perchè sei cos'ingrata
    Se sai per te son cieco
    Dolor sta sempre meco.

O Dio famme n'escire da sti guai
Cha non g'encapparaggio n'altra fiata.
    Perchè sei cos'ingrata
    Se sai per te son cieco
    Dolor sta sempre meco.

Io[3] mor'o camp'hormai non menne curo
Sto mondo latr'è fatt'a chi a ventura.
    Perchè sei cos'ingrata
    Se sai per te son cieco
    Dolor sta sempre meco.

(My lady, I don't know why you do it.
Why are you always so angry about everything?
Why are you so ungrateful?
You know because of you I'm blind
And always filled with heartache.

I don't know what's come into your head;
I do know that you'd love to make me die.
Why are you so ungrateful?
You know because of you I'm blind
And always filled with heartache.

Oh God, let me out of such troubles,
Because I can't live with them another moment.
Why are you so ungrateful?
You know because of you I'm blind
And always filled with heartache.

I don't give a damn by now if I live or die;
One needs luck to make it in this world of thieves.
Why are you so ungrateful?
You know because of you I'm blind
And always filled with heartache.)

TEXT:
1. N1545/1Ga: melle.
2. ciocchie: Neapolitan for cervello (Mal.P, I, 648).
3. N1545/1Ga: Ho.

MUSIC: Mm. 1-7, 11-14, cantus, and mm. 6-7, 12-13, tenor, are obliterated in the source; they are reconstructed from CW, VIII, 13 (transcribed from N1541Sc). The music to "Dolor, dolor sta sempre meco" is repeated in N1541Sc (cf. CW, VIII, 13). Mod. eds. in CW, VIII, 13; NolaO, I, 91.

[23] *O Dio se vede chiaro ch'io per te moro* (Nola) [Gian Domenico da Nola] Source: N1545/1Ga

O Dio se vede chiaro ch'io per te moro
Perchè me straci oime[1] sì fieramente.
    Mirati o gente
    Come me tratta mal questa crudele.

De[2] perchè voi ch'io pasma in tal martoro
Se viver mi poi far sì dolcemente.
    Mirati o gente
    Come me tratta mal questa crudele.

Meschino me sai bene quant'io th'adoro[3]
E penar me voi far sì stranamente.
    Mirati o gente
    Come me tratta mal questa crudele.

Dhe per pietà o vita de la mia vita
Donnam'a[4] me ch'io th'amo[5] qualche aita.[6]
    Mirati o gente
    Come me tratta mal questa crudele.[7]

(Oh God! It's so obvious that I'm dying for you,
Why must you tear at me so fiercely?
    Look everyone,
    See how badly this cruel woman treats me.

Alas! Why do you want me to suffer such torment
When you can improve my life so sweetly?
    Look everyone,
    See how badly this cruel woman treats me.

I'm so miserable! You know well how much I adore you,
And yet you make me suffer so outlandishly.
    Look everyone,
    See how badly this cruel woman treats me.

For pity's sake! Life of my life
Give some help to the one who so adores you.
    Look everyone,
    See how badly this cruel woman treats me.)

TEXT: N1545/1Ga, Q1566Sc—4 strophes.
1. Q1566Sc: strac'oime.
2. Q1566Sc: Dhe.
3. Q1566Sc: t'adoro.
4. Q1566Sc: donam'a.
5. Q1566Sc: t'amo.
6. Q1566Sc: qualch'aita.
7. Q1566Sc: the refrain changes to "O dolce vita/acciò la doglia mia te sia gradita" (Dearest heart, I wish you could appreciate my suffering).

MUSIC: M. 4, all parts, beat 3, rest omitted in Q1566Sc; bassus, vertical bar at the end of the first verse line; cantus and tenor, repeat sign at the end of the first verse line in Q1556Sc. M. 9, all parts, mensuration sign is 3 with coloration in N1545/1Ga, Q1566Sc. M. 10, all parts, mensuration sign is C in N1545/1Ga, Q1566Sc. M. 12, cantus, vertical bar after "fieramente" in Q1566Sc. M. 13, tenor, vertical bar after "mirati" in Q1566Sc. M. 17, tenor and bassus, vertical bar after "gente" in Q1566Sc. On the meaning of these vertical bars, see Card.C, 184. Mm. 20 and 24, tenor, note 1 is a minim in Q1566Sc. M. 27 is identical to m. 23 in Q1566Sc. Mod. ed. in NolaO, I, 107.

[24] *O dolce vita mia che t'haggio fatto* (Nola) [Gian Domenico da Nola] Source: N1545/2Ga

O dolce vita mia che t'haggio[1] fatto
Che me menaz'ogn'hor[2] con[3] toi parole.
    Et io mi strugo come nev'al sole.

Se sai per tuo amor son quasi matto
Ch'a tte de l'ardor mio niente te dole.
    Et io mi strugo come nev'al sole.

Mo son perduto et tengomi disfatto[4]
Che m'ai[5] mandat'a coglier le viole.
    Et io mi strugo come nev'al sole.

Questo è più vero che non è lo[6] specchio
Che l'amor[7] novo sempre caccia il vecchio.
    Et io mi strugo come nev'al sole.

(Sweet life of mine, what have I done
That makes you constantly threaten me?
    Like snow in the sun I am ever more consumed.

You must know that I'm almost crazy for love of you
Since my burning desire causes you no pain.
    Like snow in the sun I am ever more consumed.

Now I'm lost and I know I'm undone
Because you've sent me out to pick posies.
Like snow in the sun I am ever more consumed.

This proverb is more reliable than a mirror:
A new love always kicks out the old.
Like snow in the sun I am ever more consumed.)

TEXT: N1545/2Ga, Q1566Sc—4 strophes.
1. N1545/2Ga: t'aggio when the verse line is repeated; CW, VIII, 12 (according to N1541Sc): t'agio.
2. N1545/2Ga: ognior (cantus only); CW, VIII, 12: ognor.
3. CW, VIII, 12: co.
4. CW, VIII, 12: diffatto.
5. CW, VIII, 12: ch'mai.
6. CW, VIII,12: ch' ne il; Q1566Sc: che ne il.
7. N1545/2Ga, Q1566Sc: Ch'amor.

MUSIC: Mm. 1-6, all parts, no repeat of first strain in CW, VIII, 12. Mod. eds. in CW, VIII, 12; Ein.IM, III, 86; NolaO, I, 126.

Lute Intabulations

[25] *A quando a quando havea* [Adrian Willaert/Giulio Abondante] Source: A1548Sc

Vocal model: see no. [1].
Mod. ed. in Chil.L, 250.

[26] *Madonna io non lo so* [Adrian Willaert/Domenico Bianchini] Source: B1546Ga

Vocal model: see no. [7].

[27] *Madonna mia fami bona offerta* [Adrian Willaert/Giulio Abondante] Source: A1548Sc

Vocal model: see no. [5].
Mod. eds. in Chil.L, 249; EM, 654.

[28] *Madonn'io non lo so perchè lo fai* [Adrian Willaert/Giulio Abondante] Source: A1548Sc

Vocal model: see no. [7].

[29] *Vecchie retrose* [Adrian Willaert/Giulio Abondante] Source: A1548Sc

Vocal model: see no. [19], "Vecchie letrose"; "retrose" is an alternate spelling for "letrose" (see also W1544Sc).

Intabulations for Voice and Vihuela

[30] *A quand'a quand'haveva una vicina* [Adrian Willaert/Diego Pisador] Source: P1552/7Pi

Vocal model: see no. [1].
The following instruction is given at the beginning of the composition: "Otra villanesca entona se [la boz que se canta en] la prima en segundo traste" (Another villanesca: sound the singer's pitch on the first course, second fret).
MUSIC: M. 18, voice, note 1 is g'.

[31] *Madonna mia famme bon'offerta* [Adrian Willaert/Diego Pisador] Source: P1552/7Pi

Vocal model: see no. [5].
The following instruction is given at the beginning of the composition: "Otra villanesca y entona se la boz [que se canta en] la prima en segundo traste" (Another villanesca: sound the singer's pitch on the first course, second fret).
MUSIC: Mm. 18-19, voice, text underlay has "li fa nascer."

[32] *O bene mio famm'uno favore* [Adrian Willaert/Diego Pisador] Source: P1552/7Pi

Vocal model: see no. [9].
The following instruction is given at the beginning of the composition: "Otra villanesca y entosa [*sic*] [se] la boz que se canta en la segunda en tercero traste" (Another villanesca: sound the singer's pitch on the second course, third fret).
MUSIC: M. 7, voice, note 1 is g'. M. 14, notes 1-2, text underlay has "trona" here.

CANTVS

CANZONE VILLANESCHE

ALLA NAPOLITANA DI M. ADRIANO

VVIGLIARET A QVATRO VOCI

con le Canzone di Ruzante.

Con la gionta di alcune altre canzone villanesche alla napolitana di Francesco filuestrino ditto chechin et di francesco cortecia nouamente stampate con le sue stanze.

PRIMO LIBRO

A QVATRO VOCI

Venetijs Apud Antonium Gardane.
M. D. XXXXV.

Plate I. Adrian Willaert, *Canzone villanesche alla napolitana* (Venice: A. Gardane, 1545). Title page of cantus partbook. (Courtesy of Bayerische Staatsbibliothek, Munich)

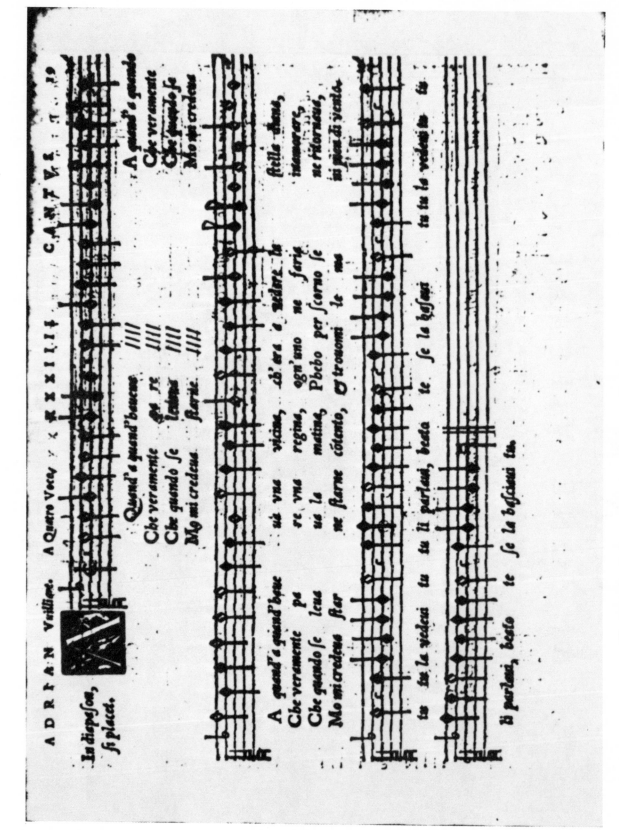

Plate II. *Madrigali a quatro voce di Geronimo Scotto* (Venice: G. Scotto, 1542).
Willaert, "A quand'a quand'haveva," cantus part.
(Courtesy of Bibliothèque Royale Albert Iᵉʳ, Brussels)

CANZONE VILLANESCHE ALLA NAPOLITANA
AND VILLOTTE

[1] A quand'a quand'haveva una vicina

Adrian Willaert

Ch'e-ra a ve-de-re la _____ stel-la Di-a-na. Tu tu la ve-de-vi
O-gnu-no ne fa-ri-a _____ i-na-mo-ra-re.
Phe-bo per scor-no se _____ ne ri-tor-na-va.
Et tro-vo-mi le ma- _____ ni pien di ven-to.

Ch'e-ra a ve-de-re la _____ stel-la Di-a-na. Tu tu la ve-de-vi
O-gnu-no ne fa-ri-a _____ i-na-mo-ra-re.
Phe-bo per scor-no se _____ ne ri-tor-na-va.
Et tro-vo-mi le ma- _____ ni pien di ven-to.

Ch'e-ra a ve-de-re la stel-la Di-a-na. Tu tu la ve-de-vi
O-gnu-no ne fa-ria i-na-mo-ra-re.
Phe-bo per scor-no se ne ri-tor-na-va.
Et tro-vo-mi le ma- ni pien di ven-to.

Ch'e-ra a ve-de-re la _____ stel-la Di-a-na. Tu tu la ve-de-vi
O-gnu-no ne fa-ri-a _____ i-na-mo-ra-re.
Phe-bo per scor-no se _____ ne ri-tor-na-va.
Et tro-vo-mi le ma- ni pien di ven-to.

tu Tu li par-la-vi Be-a-to te se la ba-scia-vi tu, Tu la ve-de-vi
tu Tu li par-la-vi Be-a-to te se la ba-scia-vi tu, Tu la ve-de-vi
tu Tu li par-la-vi Be-a-to te se la ba-scia-vi tu, Tu la ve-de-vi
tu Tu li par-la-vi Be-a-to te se la ba-scia-vi tu, Tu la ve-de-vi

tu Tu li par-la-vi Be-a-to te se la ba-scia-vi tu.
tu Tu li par-la-vi Be-a-to te se la ba-scia-vi tu.
tu Tu li par-la-vi Be-a-to te se la ba-scia-vi tu.
tu Tu li par-la-vi Be-a-to te se la ba-scia-vi tu.

[2] Buccucia dolce chiù che canamielle

Perissone Cambio

La-bruc-cia d'u-na pam- pa- na di ro- sa. Hai scro-po-lo-
Non ti mo-strar ver me tan- to sde- gno- sa.
Bo-cha ba-scia- ta mai per- de ven- tu- ra.

d'u-na pam-pa-na di ro- sa, di ro- sa. Hai scro-po-lo-
-strar ver me tan-to sde- gno- sa, sde-gno- sa.
-scia-ta mai per-de ven- tu- ra, ven-tu- ra.

-bruc-cia d'u- na pam- pa-na di ro- sa. Hai scro-po- lo- sa, hai scro- po-
ti mo-strar ver me tan-to sde-gno- sa.
-cha ba-scia- ta mai per-de ven-tu- ra.

d'u- na pam-pa-na di ro- sa, di ro- sa. Hai scro-po-lo- sa,
-strar ver me tan-to sde- gno- sa, sde-gno- sa.
-scia-ta mai per-de ven- tu- ra, ven-tu- ra.

- sa S'io cer-co un ba- so, [s'io cer- co un ba- so] Ri-

-sa S'io cer-co un ba- so, [s'io cer-co un ba- so] Ri-spon-

-lo- sa S'io cer-co un ba- so, [s'io cer- co un ba- so] Ri-

scro-po-lo- sa S'io cer-co un ba- so, [s'io cer- co un ba- so] Ri-

-spon-di: ba ca mar-zo te l'a ra- so, [ba ca mar-zo te l'a ra- so.]

- di: ba ca mar-zo te l'a ra- so, [ba ca mar-zo te l'a ra- so.]

-spon-di: ba ca mar-zo te l'a ra- so, [ba ca mar-zo te l'a ra- so.]

- spon-di: ba ca mar-zo te l'a ra- so, [ba ca mar-zo te l'a ra- so.]

[3] Cingari simo venit'a giocare

Adrian Willaert

8

[4] Le vecchie per invidia sono pazze

Francesco Corteccia

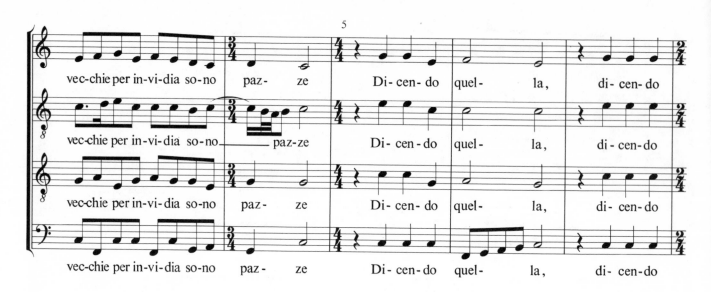

vec-chie per in-vi-dia so-no paz- ze Di-cen-do quel- la, di- cen-do

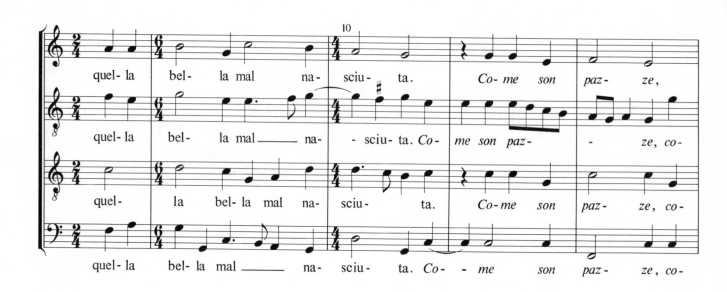

quel- la bel- la mal na- sciu- ta. Co-me son paz- ze,

co- me son paz-ze Ste vec-chie ca- naz- ze, Co- me son

[5] Madonna mia famme bon'offerta

Adrian Willaert

[6] Madonna mia io son un poverello

Anonymous

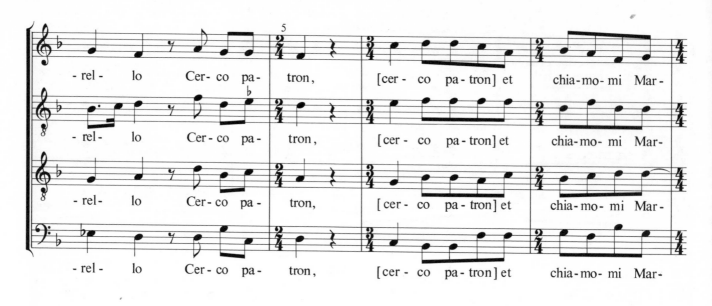

-rel- lo Cer-co pa- tron, [cer- co pa-tron] et chia-mo-mi Mar-

-rel- lo Cer-co pa- tron, [cer- co pa-tron] et chia-mo-mi Mar-

-rel- lo Cer-co pa- tron, [cer- co pa-tron] et chia-mo-mi Mar-

-rel- lo Cer-co pa- tron, [cer- co pa-tron] et chia-mo-mi Mar-

-ti- no. Co- me son fi- no Pro-va-m'un po- co per o-gni

-ti- no. Co- me son fi- no Pro-va-m'un po- co per o- gni

-ti- no. Co- me son fi- no Pro-va-m'un po- co per o-gni

-ti- no. Co-me son fi- no Pro-va-m'un po- co per o- gni

lo- co Co-me ti ser- vo da se- r'et mat- ti- no Et chia-mo-mi Mar-

lo- co Co-me ti ser- vo da se- r'et mat- ti- no Et chia-mo-mi Mar-

lo- co Co-me ti ser- vo da se- r'et mat- ti- no Et chia-mo-mi Mar-

lo- co Co-me ti ser- vo da se- r'et mat- ti- no Et chia-mo-mi Mar-

[7] Madonn'io non lo so perchè lo fai

Adrian Willaert

[8] Madonn'io t'haggi amat'et amo assai

Francesco Corteccia

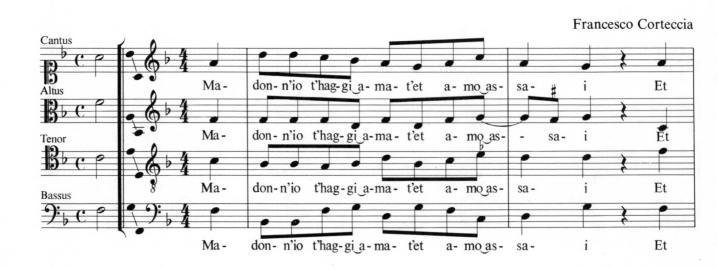

mai non mi vo- le- sti con- so- la- re   Et sem- pre d'og- g'in cra- i.

mai non mi vo- le- sti con- so- la- re   Et sem- pre d'og- g'in cra- i.

mai non mi vo- le- sti con- so- la- re   Et sem- pre d'og- g'in cra- i.

mai non mi vo- le- sti con- so- la- re   Et sem- pre d'og- g'in cra- i.

Cra cra   cra cra   cra   cra cra   cra   cra   cra cra cra fa la cor-

Cra cra cra cra   cra   cra   cra cra   cra   cra   cra cra fa la cor-

Cra cra cra cra   cra   cra cra cra   cra cra   cra cra cra cra fa la cor-

Cra cra cra cra   cra   cra cra cra   cra cra   cra cra cra cra fa la cor-

- na- chia Et al- le pe- ne mia fi- ne non sac- chia,   Et sem- pre d'og- g'in

- na- chia Et al- le pe- ne mia fi- ne non sac- chia,   Et sem- pre d'og- g'in

- na- chia Et al- le pe- ne mia fi- ne non sac- chia,   Et sem- pre d'og- g'in

- na- chia Et al- le pe- ne mia fi- ne non sac- chia,   Et sem- pre d'og- g'in

[9] O bene mio fam'uno favore

Adrian Willaert

[10] O Dio si vede chiaro cha per te moro

Francesco Silvestrino

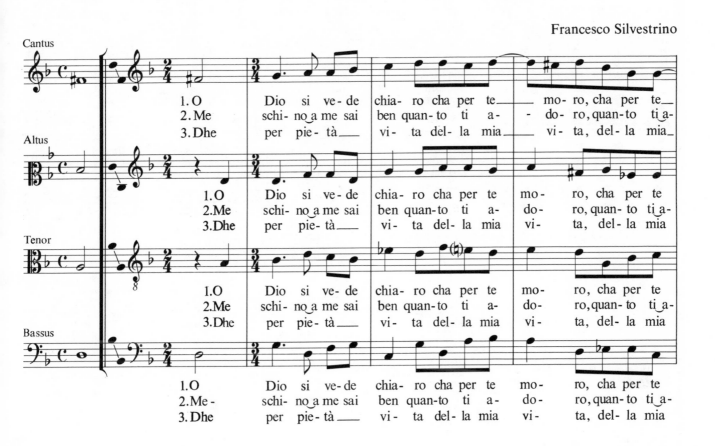

[11] O dolce vita mia che t'haggio fatto

Adrian Willaert

[12] Occhio non fu giamai che lachrimasse

Adrian Willaert

30

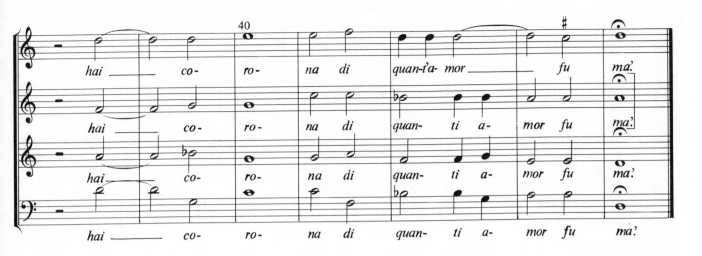

[13] Quando di rose d'oro

Adrian Willaert

[14] Se mille volte ti vengh'a vedere

Francesco Silvestrino

34

[15] Sempre mi ride sta donna da bene

Adrian Willaert

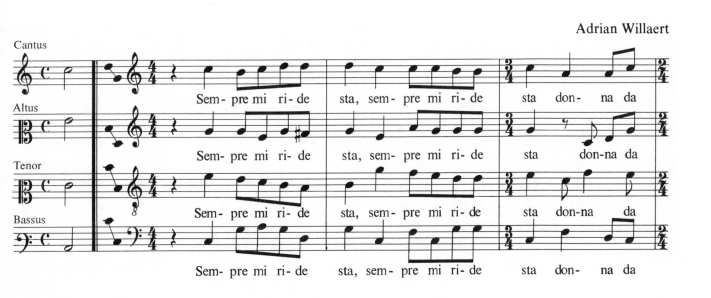

36

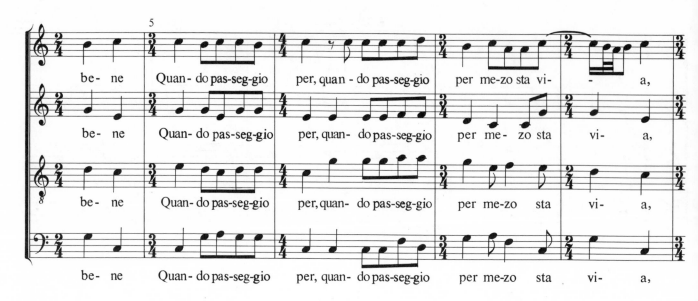

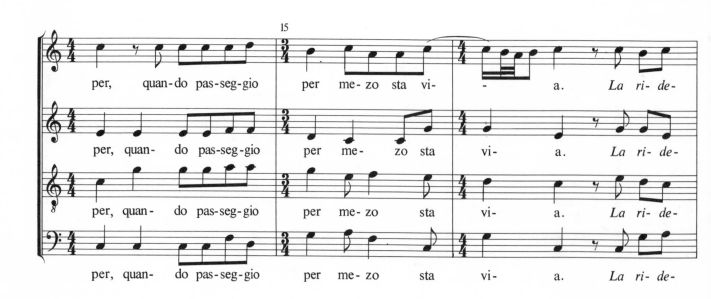

[16] Si come bella sei fosti pietosa

Francesco Silvestrino

[17] Sospiri miei d'oime dogliorirosi et senz'aita

Adrian Willaert

Deh par-ti-te-vi da me can-gia-te lo-co, Deh par-ti-te-vi da

me can-gia-te lo-co. Do che ti gio-va (do ri don) es-ser sì

bel-la Son (fa ru ra ru rel-la) vuoi be-n'a me. Do che ti gio-va

[18] Un giorno mi pregò una vedovella

Adrian Willaert

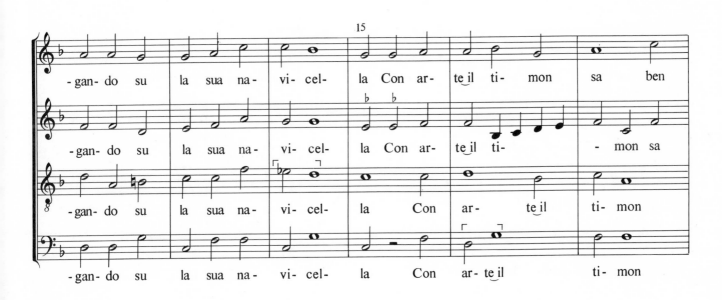

46

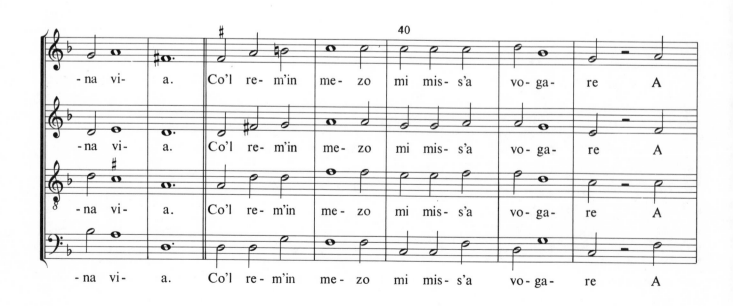

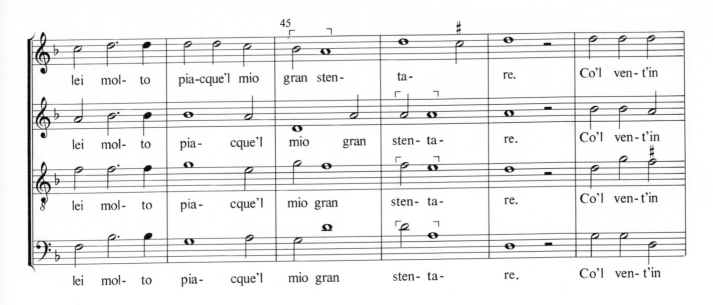

lei mol- to pia-cque'l mio gran sten- ta- re. Co'l ven- t'in

lei mol- to pia- cque'l mio gran sten- ta- re. Co'l ven- t'in

lei mol- to pia- cque'l mio gran sten- ta- re. Co'l ven- t'in

lei mol- to pia- cque'l mio gran sten- ta- re. Co'l ven- t'in

pop- pa pen- sai d'a- ne- ga- re Ma m'ai- u- tò da Ber- ghem mio

pop- pa pen- sai d'a- ne- ga- re Ma m'ai- u- tò da Ber- ghem mio

pop- pa pen- sai d'a- ne- ga- re Ma m'ai- u- tò da Ber- ghem mio com-

pop- pa pen- sai d'a- ne- ga- re Ma m'ai- u- tò da Ber- ghem mio

com- pa- re, ma m'ai- u- tò da Ber- ghem mio com- pa- re. Et

com- pa- re, ma m'ai- u- tò da Ber- ghem mio com- pa- re. Et

-pa- re, ma m'ai- u- tò da Ber- ghem mio com- pa- re. Et

com- pa- re, ma m'ai- u- tò da Ber- ghem mio com- pa- re. Et

so- spi-ran-do dis- si Deh_____ ca- ____ ra ve-do- vel- la Co- ___ sì trat-

so- spi-ran-do dis- si Deh, deh ca- ___ ra ve-do- vel- la Co- ___ sì trat-

so- spi-ran-do dis- si Deh, deh ca- __ ra ve-do- vel- la Co- ___ sì trat-

so- spi-ran-do dis- si Deh_____ ca- ___ ra ve-do- vel- la Co- ___ sì trat-

-ti gl'a-mi- ci Su la_____ tua na-vi- -cel- la, Co- sì

-ti gl'a-mi- ci Su la_____ tua ____ na- vi-cel- la, Co- sì

-ti gl'a-mi- ci Su la____ tua na- -vi-cel- la, Co- sì

-ti gl'a-mi- ci Su la_____ tua na-vi- cel- la, Co- sì

trat- ti gl'a-mi- ci Su la_____ tua na- vi- cel- la.

trat- ti gl'a- mi- ci Su la_____ tua_____ na- vi-cel- la.

trat- ti gl'a- mi- ci Su la tua na- vi- cel- la.

trat- ti gl'a-mi- ci Su la tua na-vi-cel- __ la.

[19] Vecchie letrose non valete niente

Adrian Willaert

50

[20] Zoia zentil che per secreta via

Adrian Willaert

La canzon di Ruzante

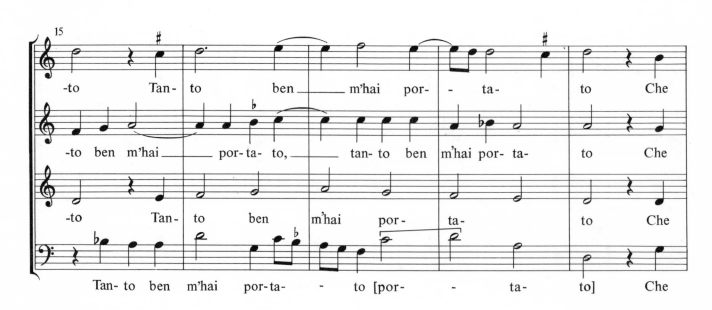

per le-grez-za tan- ta El m'è for- za che can- ta, [El

m'è for- za che can- ta:] Fa li le li lon, [fa li

le li lon,] fa li le li la li lon, fa li le li lon, [fa li le li

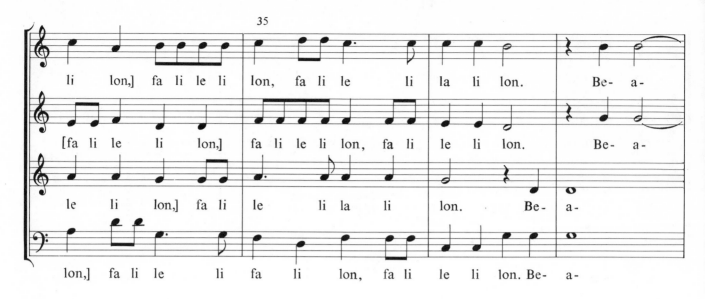

li lon,] fa li le li lon, fa li le li la li lon. Be- a-

[fa li le li lon,] fa li le li lon, fa li le li lon. Be- a-

le li lon,] fa li le li la li lon. Be- a-

lon,] fa li le li fa li lon, fa li le li lon. Be- a-

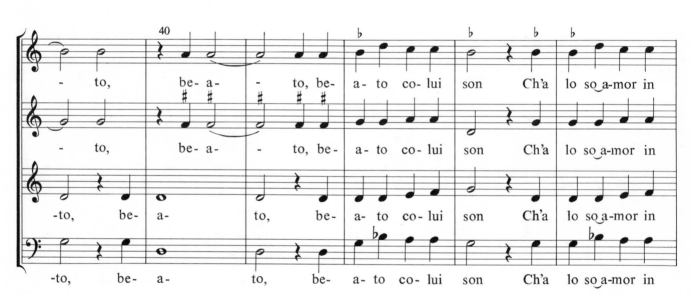

- to, be- a- - to, be- a- to co- lui son Ch'a lo so a- mor in

- to, be- a- - to, be- a- to co- lui son Ch'a lo so a- mor in

-to, be- a- to, be- a- to co- lui son Ch'a lo so a- mor in

-to, be- a- to, be- a- to co- lui son Ch'a lo so a- mor in

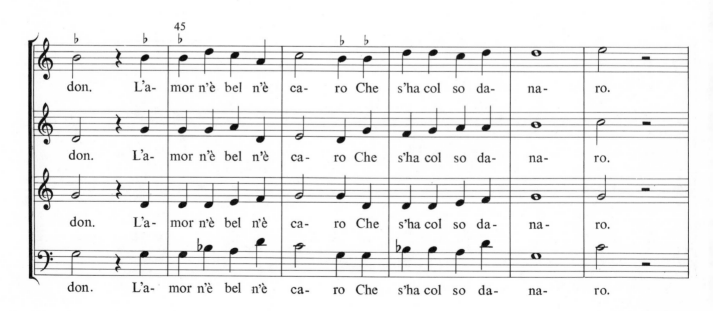

don. L'a- mor n'è bel n'è ca- ro Che s'ha col so da- na- ro.

don. L'a- mor n'è bel n'è ca- ro Che s'ha col so da- na- ro.

don. L'a- mor n'è bel n'è ca- ro Che s'ha col so da- na- ro.

don. L'a- mor n'è bel n'è ca- ro Che s'ha col so da- na- ro.

[21] Cingari simo venit'a giocare

Gian Domenico da Nola

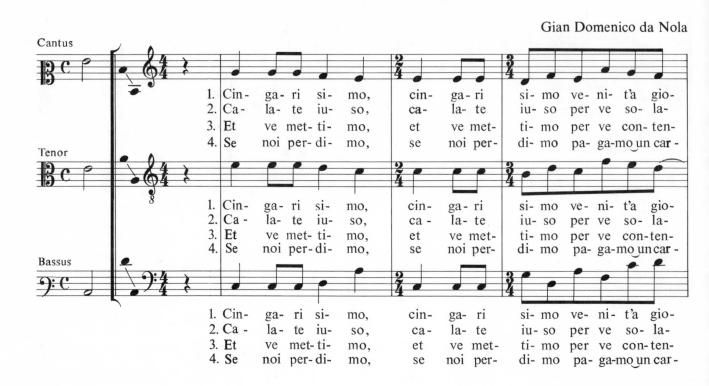

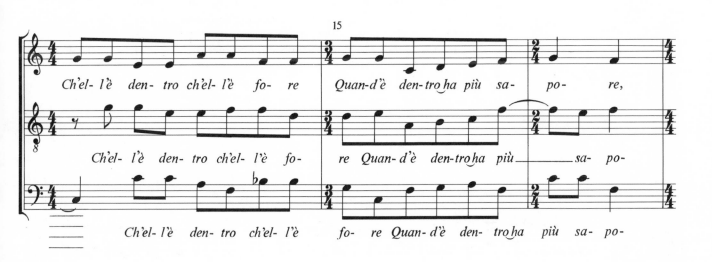

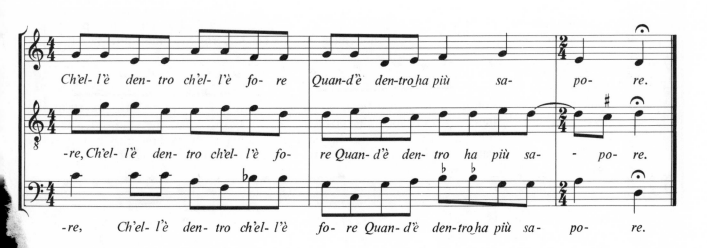

[22] Madonn'io non lo so perchè lo fai

Gian Domenico da Nola

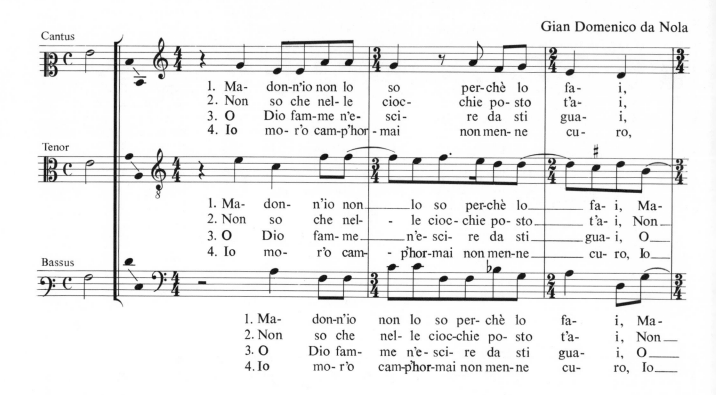

[23] O Dio se vede chiaro ch'io per te moro

Gian Domenico da Nola

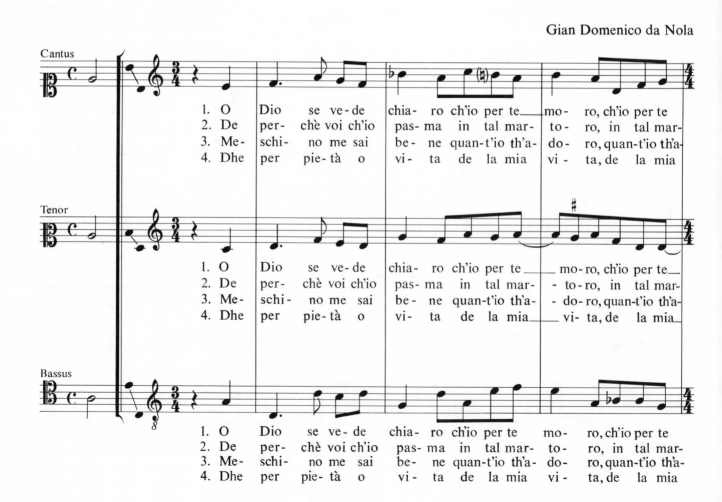

[24] O dolce vita mia che t'haggio fatto

Gian Domenico da Nola

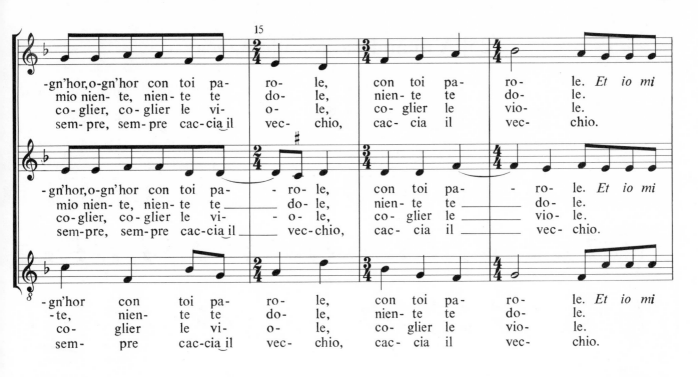

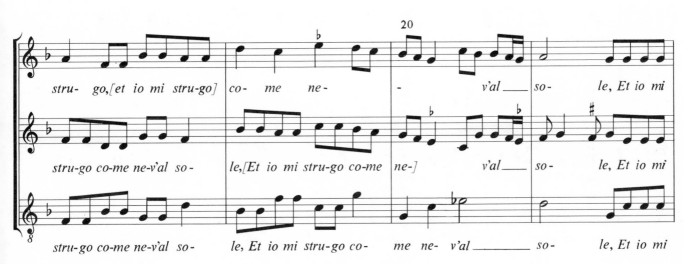

[25] A quando a quando havea

Adrian Willaert / Giulio Abondante

[26] Madonna io non lo so

Adrian Willaert / Domenico Bianchini

[27] Madonna mia fami bona offerta

Adrian Willaert / Giulio Abondante

[28] Madonn'io non lo so perchè lo fai

Adrian Willaert / Giulio Abondante

[29] Vecchie retrose

Adrian Willaert / Giulio Abondante

[30] A quand'a quand'haveva una vicina

Adrian Willaert / Diego Pisador

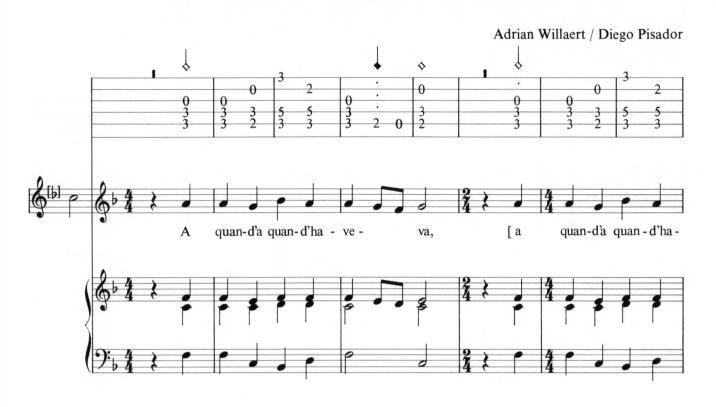

A quan-d'a quan-d'ha - ve - va, [a quan-d'a quan-d'ha-

- ve - va,] a quan-d'a quan-do, a quan-d'a quan-d'ha-ve - va u - na vi-ci - na

Ch'e-ra a ve-de - re la _____ stel - la Di - a - na. *Tu tu la ve-de-vi*

tu Tu li par-la - vi Be - a - to te se la ba-scia-vi tu, Tu la ve-de-vi

[31] Madonna mia famme bon'offerta

Adrian Willaert / Diego Pisador

Ch'io por-to per pre - sen - te sto ga - luc - cio, ch'io por-to per pre - sen - te sto ga -

-luc - cio. *Che sem-pre can - ta, [che sem-pre can - ta] quan- d'è dì al - le gal-*

-li- ne, [al- le gal-li-ne] E di - ce: chi chir chi [chi chir chi chi chir chi] [chi chir

chi E] tan-to cal-ca for- te, e tan-to cal-ca for- te la gal- li - na Che li fa na-scer

l'o- v'o-gni mat— —ti-na, [che li fa na-scer l'o-v'o-gni mat— —ti-na.]

[32] O bene mio famm'uno favore

Adrian Willaert / Diego Pisador

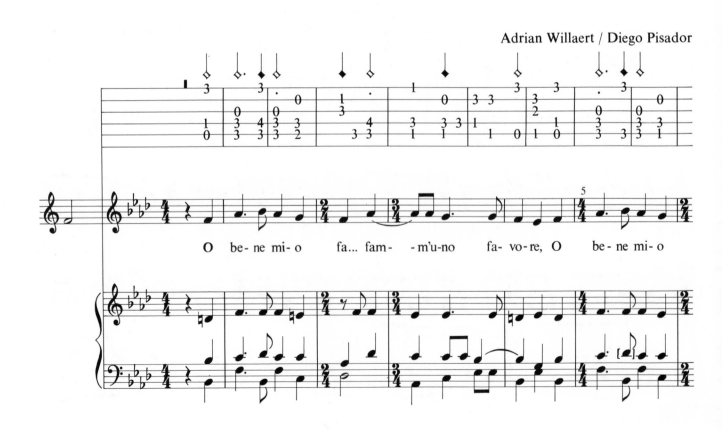

O be-ne mi-o fa... fam— —m'u-no fa-vo-re, O be-ne mi-o

fa... fam- -m'u-no fa- vo- re Che que- sta se- ra ti pos-sa par-la- re, ti pos-sa par-

-la- re. E s'al- cu- no ti ci tro- va E tu gri- da, e tu gri- da: chi ven-

-d'o- va, chi ven- d'o- va, chi ven- d'o- va, E s'al- cu- no ti ci tro- va E tu

gri- da, e tu gri- da: chi ven- d'o- va, chi ven- d'o- va, chi ven- d'o- va.